PLUNKED

PLUNKED

MICHAEL NORTHROP

SCHOLASTIC PRESS

NEW YORK

Library of Congress Cataloging-in-Publication Data

Northrop, Michael.
Plunked / Michael Northrop. — 1st ed.
p. cm.
Summary: Sixth-grader Jack Mogens loses his nerve after getting hit by a pitch,
and has to dig deep within himself to avoid giving up the sport he loves.
[1. Baseball — Fiction. 2. Schools — Fiction. 3. Fear — Fiction. 4. Perseverance
(Ethics) — Fiction.]

PZ7.N8185Pl 2012
[Fic]—dc23
2011032737

ISBN 978-0-545-29714-1

10 9 8 7 6 5 4 3 2 1   12 13 14 15 16

Printed in the U.S.A.   23

First edition,
March 2012

The text was set in Sabon MT.
Book design by
Christopher
Stengel

For Neil Cohen, who gave a cub
reporter a break (a few, actually)

Part I
DIGGING IN

Chapter 1

Jackson hits an absolute bomb to deep center field. The bat makes a *PING* that could shatter glass. Jackson is one of our best hitters, and that's his best shot of the day. Coach Wainwright has seen enough.

"Next batter!" he shouts.

That's me. My name is Jack Mogens, and I'm a sixth grader at Tall Pines Elementary. I pass Jackson and we bump fists.

"Think you just brought down a satellite," I say.

"Hope my TV still works," he says.

It's Thursday night at Culbreath Field, and Little League practice is in full swing. Jackson grabs his big first baseman's mitt and heads back into the field, and I take my place at the plate.

Coach is ready to go on the mound, but he gives me

a little time to get set. You've got to have a routine. All the big leaguers on TV do, so I do, too. First, I sort of dig my front foot in. I bat right-handed, like most kids, so my left foot is out front, and I twist my toes into the dirt a few times. Then I settle my weight onto my back foot. They always say: Sit down on the back leg. So that's what I do.

Next, I take four swings, two fast and two slow. That way, when the pitch comes, I won't be *too* fast or *too* slow! At least that's the idea. I'm still kind of working out the kinks.

Coach Wainwright has run out of patience on the mound. As soon as I look up, he lobs one in. He calls them lollipops, batting-practice fastballs. But he's three times the size of the kids who'd normally be pitching to me, so there's still something on them. And by "three times," I don't mean he's seventeen feet tall. I'm talking sheer bulk here. Coach throws left-handed, and he's one hefty lefty.

The pitch is headed my way. I squint down hard, trying to pick up the rotation of the ball so I can see where it's going. It's coming in on me, cutting in toward my body. I hate it when it does that, and OK, maybe I bail out a little. I push my body back out of the way as I push my arms forward. That's a recipe for a weak ground ball, which is exactly what I hit.

The ball dribbles pathetically down the line. Jackson, already back at his usual spot at first base, has to wait on it to arrive.

"Come on, Mogens!" Coach yells from behind his little pitching screen. "That pitch was barely inside. You've got to stay in there. I'm not gonna hit ya!"

I know, I know, I think. I just don't like the ball coming at me like that. I like the outside pitches. It's easier to extend my arms on those.

There's nothing for it now. Jackson tosses the ball back to the mound, and I dig in for the next pitch.

This one is on the outside half, and I scald it into right field. Hitting the ball to right is like gold in Little League. I mean, no offense to anyone, but they always put the worst fielders in right.

"That's the ticket!" yells Coach.

I let the smallest smile slip onto my face and dig in again. I need a few more of these before my turn is up. This is my sixth year of Little League, if you count T-ball, and my second in majors. I want to be the starter in left field. That's a big deal here. Our roster is maxed out for the second straight year, and there's really only one spot up for grabs in the outfield. My defense is there, my arm's OK, so this is what's left. I've got to get the job done with my bat and turn these lollipops around.

Once my turn is up, I head out into the field. This isn't really the time to show off your glove because there are extra fielders out here, waiting their turn at bat. You can't run and show any range without crashing into the next kid. That's OK, though. We'll shag fly balls later. For now, I settle in and wait for anything hit right at me. And I do some thinking, too. What am I going to do with those inside pitches?

Pretty soon, batting practice is over, and we all head in for the next thing. We can see Coach setting up at home plate with a bat in his hand, so we know we're working on sliding again.

"Lawsuit drill," I say to Andy as I catch up with him.

He turns around with a big, doofy smile on his face and says, "Hope no one gets killed."

Andy Rossiter is my best friend on the team. Scratch that: Andy Rossiter is my best friend, period. He has been since second grade. He's got a decent shot at starting at third this season. That's our goal: me starting in left, him at the hot corner. We're not taking no for an answer.

We laugh at "lawsuit drill," but it's kind of a nervous laugh. By the time Assistant Coach Liu starts lining us up at third, no one is even smiling. No one likes the lawsuit drill, or, as Coach Wainwright calls it, "Learning to slide! Why is it so hard for you dumb monkeys?"

The brave kids at the front of the line are pushing

through the pile of batting helmets, looking for the ones that fit them. We've been practicing for a few weeks now, so we're starting to recognize the helmets we like from the dings and dents and scuff marks on them. We're also starting to realize how those dings and dents and scuff marks got there.

We're all "Brave" kids, in one way: Our team is the Tall Pines Braves. It's just that some of us are braver than others. One by one, the first group of kids takes off from third, heading for home. Coach is standing by the plate, facing down the line. Right before they get there, he takes a little swing with that aluminum bat of his.

He swings it slow, like he's pushing it through water. And yeah, he could probably pull it back if you weren't going to make it. But Coach gets distracted sometimes, and I've only got one skull.

Anyway, that's why we call it the lawsuit drill, even though I'm pretty sure our parents signed away all of our rights as human beings on that permission form. Either way, it's really, really important to slide in time.

Right now, Katie Bowe is going. And I know what you're thinking: You've got a girl on your majors team? Yeah, and she's probably going to be our starting shortstop. She's also one of the first ones down the line and slides a good two feet under Coach's swing. She pops up in a cloud of dirt and ponytail: Safe!

The line's moving now, and there's not one kid who doesn't swallow hard waiting for his turn. Coach hasn't smacked anyone's head back to third yet. Then again, we've been practicing for less than a month. It's my turn. I double-check my helmet and race down the line.

Chapter

2

Practice is over until Saturday, when we're going to hit the batting cages in Haven. My head is still attached, but there's a decent chance I'll die in a car crash on the way home. Dad is just not paying attention. He's driven these same few roads all his life, and I guess he feels like he doesn't need to look anymore. I don't agree at all. I always buckle up, first thing, when he's driving. If I still had a batting helmet, I'd put it on.

There isn't a lot of traffic in Tall Pines at night, but there isn't none. And here's my dad, fiddling with the radio and then making way too much eye contact. Don't get me wrong: It's polite to look at the person you're talking to. It's just maybe not such a great idea while you're driving. But here he is, looking at me when he asks a question and looking over when I answer. I keep my answers short.

"How's Wainwright?" he says.

And then he half answers his own question with: "Can't believe he's still out there coaching."

"He's good," I say, and then pause so Dad will look back at the road.

He corrects his course a little, pulls the tires back off the double yellow line, then looks back toward me: "Yeah?"

"Bigger than last year," I say. And, whatever, it's true. It's getting pretty noticeable.

Dad looks back at the road. There's a good chance he'll chew me out for "judging a person by their appearance." Dad has been reading a lot of parenting books lately. I'm pretty sure that's where all of this eye contact is coming from, too. But he just cracks a smile.

"Oh, well, you know, it's not so easy for us old guys to stay slim," he says. Then he looks down at the beginning of a bulge at his belt and laughs.

"You're not old!" I say.

"I'm no spring chicken!"

Dad is always saying things like that. What is a "spring chicken," anyway? A chicken is a chicken, right? Or does a spring chicken turn into a fall turkey?

"Not old like Coach," I say. I don't really like to think of my dad getting that old — and it won't be an issue if he doesn't start looking at the road!

A car honks and he swerves back into his lane.

"Eyes on the prize," I say.

He laughs again. He loves that one, too.

"Speaking of packing on the pounds," he says, "we need to pick up dinner on the way home."

"Really?" I say, because we don't normally get takeout after practice.

"Affirmative, soldier," he says. "The orders come straight from High Command."

He means Mom.

"Where?" I ask.

"I don't know, what do you think?" he says.

Tall Pines is only an exciting place to eat if you're a termite. There are exactly three options around here at this time of the night. Still, I consider the question carefully. This is dinner we're talking about, and I'm always super hungry after practice. (Mom calls me the locust plague!)

"Well, there's pizza," I say.

"That's a good one," says dad. "Pizza at Brother's. And the Sicilian Express is always a pastability, too."

He uses the same pun every time, but I'm not really in the mood for the kind of food they make there: pasta and chicken parmesan and things like that. It's kind of a warm night, and I've been running all over the place. We finished up with sprints, and I'm sweaty and dirty in that way where the dirt is sticking to the sweat so much that you almost feel muddy.

"Seems a little fancy right now," I say, meaning I feel like the Swamp Thing. "And they always give us like seventy-two pounds of pasta."

Dad seems a little disappointed, but I point to his belt to make my point. I think he'll laugh, but he doesn't. People get touchy about that stuff. It's like it's OK for them to say, but not for anyone else.

"There's McDonald's," I say, but I guess I sort of sunk that one by pointing at his stomach, too. Dad considers the options for a few moments.

"The pizza place it is," he says, making the turnoff. "They make a mean Greek salad."

I don't understand why you would go to a pizza place and get a salad, but parents think about things differently. And it works out for me, because we can get a medium pizza (which is actually pretty large). Then Mom and Dad can just have a slice or two to go with their Greek salads, and leave the rest for me.

Anyway, we survive the decision-making process without a head-on collision.

"Make the call," Dad says, nodding to his cell phone in its little holder. It's illegal to talk on your cell while driving here, so I place the order. We pull into the lot like three minutes later. Tall Pines isn't that big a town. There's something I've noticed around here: the bigger the tree in the name, the smaller the town. "Tall Pines" . . . that's just trying too hard.

12

So we wait in Brother's for our order. There are already three other kids from the team there, and more will probably pull up. Dad stands by the counter and talks to the parents and other people he knows from town.

I go over and say hi to Tim Liu, who is Assistant Coach Liu's son. He's a nice guy, but he's locked in a pretty fierce battle at second base. His dad being a coach is kind of a problem, because if he gets it, people will grumble. I think a few kids have started the grumbling a little early, but I'm not one of them. I like Tim, and he really is a good fielder.

Then there is a younger kid named James, who I don't know that well, and Katie Bowe. It's weird with Katie. When we're at practice, she's just the shortstop. She keeps her hat pulled down low in a way that makes her look sort of tough. If it wasn't for the ponytail, you could almost forget she's a girl. But then, after practice, like literally one second after it's over, the hat comes off, and there's just no doubt.

Like right now, she has some dirt under her right eye, but it doesn't look bad the way it would on me. My hand goes up and brushes my face without me even meaning to. It's actually kind of cool on her, like it's a look or something, and a few days from now all the girls in school will be doing it.

She glances up and I look down fast. I don't think she saw. Or maybe she did. I turn back to Tim and say the first dumb thing that pops into my mind.

"Really, lot of dirt and, um, out there today," I blurt out. It's barely even a sentence.

"Huh?" he says.

I smile and shake my head, trying to think of something smart to say. Then I realize Katie is still looking over at us, so there's no chance of that.

Chapter

3

Saturday morning is like a military mission. We head to the batting cages at Hungry Hut, over in Haven. The Haven and Tall Pines leagues officially merged a while back. We're playing the Haven Yankees in our first game, so this is a trip behind enemy lines. It's like a war movie. I mean, there is pretty much no chance of gunfire, but some Haven players might see us and sort of scout us out. Or they might even be at Hungry Hut taking their own cuts in the cages.

We go early, so we can get there right when the batting cages open up at ten. There is no sign of the Craven Yankees. That's what we call them. It means cowardly. Kids on the Tall Pines team have been calling the Haven team that for forever, from back when people used words like that.

There is no sign of them or pretty much anyone else. The Hungry Hut doesn't serve breakfast, and it's pretty early for a burger and onion rings. A girl comes out and pushes up the cover of the pick-up window. She's wearing jeans and a T-shirt that says "I'm sassy! Get over it." Then she goes around to the side door and you can hear her moving stuff around inside. There's a loud thump because I guess she got too sassy and knocked something over.

Cars are pulling up one after another now, but it's all kids from our team. You get to recognize the cars after a while. Kids are spilling out the side doors of minivans and heading straight over to the cages.

Most of the cars just drop them off and then hightail it back to Tall Pines. It's Saturday morning. Most of the parents have been working all week, and now it's time to mow the lawn or go to Home Depot or Stop & Shop or whatever grown-up thing they want to cross off their list first. A few of the parents get out, though: the two assistant coaches, a few of the dads who've played ball, and a few of the moms who like to watch their kids do things like take fifteen cuts in the batting cages.

Coach Wainwright is already over at the little shack, trying to wrangle a deal from the guy who works there. The guy's name is Jimmy or Joey or something like that. I come to the cages pretty regularly during the summer, and it's pretty much always this same guy. He doesn't look completely awake yet.

Coach is doing all the talking, and Jimmy/Joey is sort of leaning back to get out of spit-spray range.

"What about some sort of bulk discount," Coach says, but not really as a question.

Jimmy/Joey looks over at us: a platoon of Tall Pines's smallest athletes. The line is long and getting longer. He looks back at Coach. "OK," he says. "Three for the price of two. But just this once."

He walks over to unlock his little shack, and Coach flashes us a big smile and a thumbs-up sign. Coach is a goofball sometimes.

Jimmy/Joey goes inside and starts dragging racks of bats and helmets out for us. Coach puts his hands up, meaning, Let the man do his job. Once he drops his hands, we swarm the racks.

All three coaches start shouting at once: "Whoa! Whoa! Whoa!" and "One at a time!" But it's like trying to stop a cattle stampede. We're elbowing each other aside and hand-fighting for the best stuff. I bulldoze my way in and am the second guy to get to the second rack of bats. You want to get a good bat and a helmet that doesn't flop around on your head or squeeze your eyes out of their sockets.

It turns out not to matter at all. Once the frenzy dies down, they make us put it all back. It's a major bummer. I'd gotten a good bat and a bad helmet, but that's still batting .500. The coaches have a point, though. Only two of us can bat at the same time, unless we want to hit in the SLOW cage like someone's grandma. So, basically, we can all take turns using the best equipment.

It makes sense, but I still grumble a little when I hand over my bat. I'd already named it Excalibur, which was King Arthur's sword and is pretty much what I always name my bats.

Anyway, we form a line alphabetically to wait for our turn. That's no prize for me: Mogens. More than half the team is ahead of me. Katie Bowe is right up front again. That's kind of good, because she makes me less nervous from a distance. She's in game mode, anyway, with her Braves cap pulled down low.

As Dad would say, you can't pick your neighbors, and Malfoy is right in front of me. That isn't his real name. His real name is Kurt Meacham, and his dad is Sam Meacham, the other assistant coach. Some of us just call him Malfoy because he looks like the blond kid from the Harry Potter movies. Also, he is a huge jerk-butt. You can't say that, though, because it could get back to his dad. Assistant Coach Meacham is an even bigger jerk-butt. It must be a family tradition.

There isn't much talking in the line. Andy is back in the Rs, too far away to talk to. We mostly just watch kids take their hacks. If anyone says anything in line, it's: "You smoked it!" or "Doink!" or whatever seems appropriate.

The pitching machine is protected by a net, but Dustin Cuddy manages to hit one right back through the square opening where the balls come out.

"Laser-guided!" yells Jackson.

The machine takes it on the nose. It makes a sound like *kull-CHIK* and does a weird little shudder.

"Everybody get down," yells Chester. "It's gonna blow!"

We all laugh, but a few seconds later, the machine lobs the next pitch out as usual. Dustin pops it up, and it's back to business.

I pay extra attention when Geoff Kass comes up. He's my main competition in left. There isn't much difference in our defense. I'm just being totally honest there. Straight up: We're about the same in the field. We're both pretty good. You know, steady, with the chance to make a really good play every now and then, maybe dive or whatever.

Our bats are going to make the difference. Last year, Geoff was a really good slap hitter. You know, he just made good contact and legged out a lot of singles. But he's grown some, and he's showing more power this season. That's good news for the team, but not for me.

Anyway, he's up now. You can't really tell how far a ball would go in a batting cage, since it just hits the net like anything else. But you can see when it's hit hard, and more than that, you can hear it. We can all hear it now.

Chester Jiménez is in the other cage. He's our best bunter, but his big thing is that he's so small, like super small. He draws a lot of walks because it's hard for pitchers to throw anything between the letters and knees on a guy that size. I've tried. It's like trying to drop a pebble into a water glass from 2,000 feet up. Chester knows it, too. He'll scrunch himself up as small as he can at the plate. He's doing it now, even though nobody ever got a walk in a batting cage.

Anyway, the point is, Chester is hitting grounders and soft liners. The sound is just *pop, pop, pop,* and there is no mistaking that for the deep, hard thuds coming from the cage next to him. Geoff is laying into 'em, the way you can in a batting cage, with no one on the mound trying to outthink you. A slow roller comes in, and *THUD!* He sends it the other way. Another one, straight and a little low; a third, higher with a little bend to it . . . It doesn't matter: *THUD! THUD! THUD!*

I can feel my palms starting to sweat a little as I watch. Pretty soon, Chester and Geoff have taken their fifteen swings. They push the cage doors open and take off their helmets, and I move up two more spots.

I'm almost there, and then I am. I adjust my helmet, take the token from Coach, and step into the cage.

Grip it and rip it.

That's what I tell myself as I work the palms of my

batting gloves across the worn black tape on the handle of the bat.

I press my left foot into the asphalt and twist it back and forth in time with my gloves. The red light on top of the pitching machine blinks on like the glowing eye of a Terminator bent on my destruction. Just like always, I start to take my four mini swings, but the first pitch comes out before I'm done.

That's the thing about pitching machines: No manners.

I rush the bat back, pick my left foot up, and step into it. I drill it, a screamer into the netting, just left of center.

That's the other thing about pitching machines: You can hit them a ton! I could hear the solid contact when Geoff was up, but now that it's my turn, I can *feel* it, too. The energy shoots from my hands right down into the ground, like electricity, but it doesn't hurt. It feels great.

I watch another dirt-smeared ball roll down and disappear into the machine. There's a little *fa-chunk* sound and out it comes, a little higher and straighter than the last one. I drill that one, too, but I chop a grounder on the third pitch.

They aren't real baseballs. They can't be, with the pounding they take. They're hard rubber with dozens of little dimples on them, like oversize, soft golf balls. The machine throws them harder or softer; sometimes they'll dip and sometimes not so much. The pitching machine is kind of a clunky thing, just a paddle that flips the ball out at you. That's why it's good: Every pitch is different, just like in a game.

Except that every pitch is more or less over the plate, something like a strike. The balls never really cut in on you too much. Even if they do, they're just hard rubber traveling medium speed. And so you can just step in and drill them. The worst thing that could happen to you is that you could swing and miss.

I do that on pitch number seven. I've hit a few scorchers in a row, and I think I just get overaggressive. That gets the mouths moving.

"Whiff!" someone yells. It's sort of distracting because you can't help but try to place the voices.

"No batta!" shouts someone else. It takes a half second but I realize it's Jackson, just kidding around.

"If you're looking for the ball," yells Manny, our center fielder, "it's a foot under your bat!"

Yeah, ha-ha-ha. I know they're just kidding, but then Malfoy chimes in. "You suck!" he yells. "Looo-ser!"

I didn't say anything when he swung and missed, like, a minute ago. But if there's a line, Malfoy will cross it. And of course he's not going to get in trouble with his dad right there.

I guess I let it get under my skin because I barely make contact on the next one and chop it into the ground. I flick my head back quickly to see if the coaches are watching. If they are, it's not that closely.

They're talking and looking up now and then. You aren't really going to impress the coaches by hitting the meatballs this thing is serving up. Plus, eight or nine kids have gone already. The coaches seem pretty well zoned out at this point, maybe just listening for that solid contact they like.

The cages are more for us, just to get our swings down and work on anything we think we need to work on.

Fa-chunk!

The next pitch is on its way and I cannot — repeat: cannot — have a third bad swing in a row. I squint down hard and concentrate on the greasy rubber orbazoid coming at me. I drill it high and hard into the net. The next one, too.

And then my fifteen pitches are up. The red eye of the machine blinks out. I hold the wire-mesh door open for the next kid. I go to put my helmet and bat away, and Andy is there, pretending to push through the racks.

"Good cuts," he says, and then cracks a smile. "For the most part!"

"Not my fault," I say. "That pitcher's pretty crafty."

"Looks to me like his arm is getting tired."

"Then you might have a chance," I tell him.

He pretends to hit me with the bat he's pretending to try out.

I put mine back in the rack. As Andy and I are walking away, one of the younger kids picks my bat right back out. He takes a few slow swings with it, testing the balance. That's a compliment, too.

I look around. Geoff is watching me, seeing which bat I used, seeing the kid pick it up. He turns away quick, but I don't mind. I've been watching him, too.

Chapter

4

We're still eating the ice cream bars that Coach bought us when our parents start to arrive. He bought them with the money he saved on the tokens. It's late March, and it's not like it's actually hot. It's just a nice, early spring day, and we have free ice cream, and it's like, who says being an athlete is hard work?

I lick the wooden stick clean and chuck it in the garbage can when I see Mom's car pull up. The Green Machine, we call it. It's pretty ugly: a stubby old Honda, and a weird shade of green. It's the kind of car people use to go to the train station and back, a "station car." Except that Mom doesn't use it for that, since she works in town. She just beats around Tall Pines in it. She isn't driving today, though. As I walk across the lot, I can see Mom in the passenger seat. Dad is driving. He kind of likes the Green Machine, too.

I climb into the tiny backseat and close the door behind me. Dad starts the car and looks over his shoulder: "How'd it go?"

I really hope he won't try to make eye contact the whole way from up there.

Mom looks back, waiting for my reply and scanning me for any signs of injury. I just smile because no one ever gets hurt in a batting cage. No one except the balls, anyway.

"OK," I say.

"Is that Siobhan over there?" Mom asks, meaning Andy's mom.

It is, but we've already pulled out of the lot. We're on our way back to town.

"Work up an appetite?" asks Dad.

"Sure!" I say. I don't tell them about the ice cream.

We decide to go to the deli counter at the supermarket because they make the best sandwiches. Mom gets a Veggie Deluxe. As near as I can tell, it's a salad between two slices of chunky brown bread. So weird.

When we pull into our driveway, I can hear Nax going crazy even before the car comes to a stop.

"Someone needs to be walked," says Mom.

Nax is barking up a storm in the kitchen. His paws are on the glass of the door, and his eyes are wild with excitement as I cross the lawn. I've only been gone a few hours, but Nax can't tell time. He's a black Lab, nothing fancy. Sometimes when he's being crazy we call him "the Lab experiment."

Nax and I go for a walk on the Rail Trail that runs along the train tracks near our house. As long as he doesn't do his business right on the pavement, I don't really need to pick up after him back there. When he was little, I used to have to drag him off to the side when he started squatting, but he mostly knows the deal by now. Sometimes he even pulls me off to the side, stretching to the end of his leash and contributing some quality fertilizer to the grass and flowers and weeds along the side of the path.

Nax is a smart dog. I mean, they say Labs are smart, in general, but I think he might be a little smarter than normal. The only reason I even use the leash anymore is because of the squirrels. He goes crazy trying to chase them. If he was an athlete, that would be his sport: the squirrelathlon. He loves it. Sometimes I'll try to run along with him, just so he can chase them for more than four feet at a time. He's never going to catch one, but he either doesn't know that or doesn't care.

"Good dog," I say as he finishes his business. He comes up, and I scratch him behind the ear, just where he likes it.

We turn around at the little pond. It used to be just a big puddle, but it has grown up just like Nax has. We have to get back because there's homework waiting. Not for Nax, of course — he's not that smart! — but for me.

They'll probably make me mow the lawn, too. It's the kind of stuff you want to fast-forward past, but you can't. This whole week is going to be like that, waiting to find out on Thursday if I'm a starter.

"Fun while it lasted," I say to Nax. Ten feet later, we take off after a squirrel.

Chapter 5

Monday mornings always suck. It's sort of a law of nature. Or a law of human nature, anyway. It's not like beavers send their kids off to some little beaver hut to learn how to build dams. That's kind of a dumb thought, but that's the kind I have when I'm lying there avoiding getting out of bed.

It's not like I completely hate school, but I'll be honest: I kind of hate it on Mondays. There's never anything I can do about it, though. I have the kind of alarm clock the whole house can hear. I think, in the town of Tall Pines, it ranks third in noise to the clock tower on the Congregational Church and the alarm horn at the Tall Pines Volunteer Fire Department.

The alarm goes off: *BRREEEEP! BRREEEEP! BRREEEEP!*

I scramble to slap the button on top. Then I throw the sheets off and get up.

I go through the same routine as always: clean up, get dressed, cereal, bus stop, bus ride, school.

I'm still sort of blinking myself awake in first period, history. History class is ridiculous even on non-Mondays. It's like the whole nation is terrified that there is some child somewhere who doesn't know about the Louisiana Purchase.

Second period is English, and at least I'm fully awake for that. We're reading *The Island of Dr. Moreau* by H. G. Wells. It's one of those really old books. I'd heard the name H. G. Wells before, but I hadn't realized he was a real person until the book plopped down on my desk. I thought he was like Sherlock Holmes or something.

The book is actually pretty cool. First of all, it's short, and those are the best kind of books. Second, it's about this crazy doctor (guess what his name is! Ha-ha!). He's creating half animal, half human creatures on this island, like a half pig or a half wolf or whatever. It's kind of a cool concept.

On the team, one of the best things you can call someone is a beast. "You're a beast, man!" Like if J.P., who's our best pitcher, strikes out ten guys, you'd say that.

Anyway, we're most of the way through the book. Like I said, it's short. There are no assigned seats in

English because Mr. Haun doesn't "believe in them." But Andy and I usually get there early enough to sit across the aisle from each other. Sometimes we sit one in front of the other in the same aisle, but that's not as good, because one of us has to turn around to talk.

Anyway, today we're across from each other, like two-thirds of the way back. Perfect location. The bell hasn't gone off yet, and we're talking about what sort of half human, half animal we'd be.

"I'd be, like, I'd be . . ." says Andy.

He's taking too long, so I start in: "Donkey! Skunk! Monkey-butt!"

"Shut up!" he says. "I think I'd be a jaguar."

"Yeah, right!" I say.

"No, seriously, think about it."

"I am. That's why I said 'yeah, right.'"

"Seriously, I'm kind of small but pretty fast."

"I think that's cheetahs," I say.

"I'm not *that* fast," says Andy, and then the bell rings.

"Half tiger!" I say quickly, in that second when everyone is opening up their notebook and straightening out in their seat.

Andy rolls his eyes, but tigers are tougher than jaguars, and it's too late for him to change his pick. Mr. Haun is already talking.

Andy and I don't have all of the same classes, but we

always meet up at lunch. Whoever gets to the caf first saves a seat. By the time I navigate my tray of Mexican Surprise through the rows, I can see that Andy is already sitting down and eating. He really is fast. Maybe not jaguar fast, but still. Tim Liu is across from him, and I slide my tray into the reserved parking spot next to him.

"What are you losers talking about?" I say.

The answer is baseball, of course. Most of the time it's about our team, but sometimes it's the big leagues. Opening day is coming up, so it's on our minds. (It's not like it wouldn't be on our minds after opening day, but you know how it is. April baseball is kind of low stakes in the majors.)

Jackson wore a Yankees hat into school this morning, and so we're talking about whether or not the Yankees are evil. I guess it would be more accurate to say we're talking about how evil the Yankees are and whether or not that makes Jackson evil, too.

"Their payroll is like a billion dollars," Tim says.

"No way," I say. "It's like two hundred–some million."

"Yuh-huh," says Tim. "I mean total, long-range. They've got those big guys on like five- and ten-year contracts at ten or twenty million a pop."

Those are what you call ballpark figures. I mean, there's a pretty big difference between five and ten years and ten million and twenty million dollars. The thing is, though, he's sort of right.

"And Kansas City pays like forty million bucks for the whole team," he adds.

I think that might be a little low, but again, ballpark.

"Evil," says Andy.

"Evil," Tim and I agree.

There's a little pause.

"The Sox are, like —" I say.

"Like two-thirds of the Yankees," says Tim.

If you just say the Sox, you mean the Red Sox. If you mean the White Sox, you have to say so. That's just the way the world works.

And then Chester plunks his tray down on the table.

"Hello, losers," he says. We use that word a lot. It's OK to call someone a loser if he's your friend. I don't know if that's the way the world works, too, or if it's just sixth grade.

Anyway, we start to bust on him about the Mexican Surprise. That probably isn't cool of us, but it doesn't matter.

"My parents are from Ecuador," says Chester. "Don't be so ignorant."

"Come on," says Andy, drawing a line from Tim to me with his finger. "You know these two can't help it."

"Chuhhh," says Tim. "You, like, *aspire* to be ignorant."

Andy makes a far-off expression with his face and goes, "Someday . . ."

We laugh, and then we start talking about the team, our team. That's always going to happen when the four of us are together.

Chapter 6

It's Monday night and my parents are going to an Awesome Eighties concert at the Atheneum. It's a forty-five-minute or thirty-year drive from here, depending on how you look at it. The show features not one, not two, but three bands I know nothing about. The funniest thing about it is seeing my parents getting all dressed up. My mom has one ancient can of hair spray that she pretty much only uses for things like this.

FFFshhhhhFFFFFshhhh! I hear through the partially open bathroom door.

Mom emerges from the bathroom with a hair cliff above her forehead and a faded T-shirt that says "The Go-Go's" on it. Her sneakers could not be any pinker.

"Lookin' good, Mom," I say, giving her a weak thumbs-up.

"Thanks," she says. "I've got the beat!"

It's doubtful, but I don't say so. Then I turn the corner and see Dad in a polo shirt the color of pistachio ice cream — or the insides of that one kind of squashed caterpillar. He has the tip of each side of his collar pinched between the thumb and first finger of his hands. "What do you think," he says, "up or down?"

"Oh, Dad," I say, shaking my head.

A moment later, Mom comes around the corner.

"Up or down?" he repeats.

"Pop it!" she says.

He raises the collar up so that it's like the top of a squashed-caterpillar-green cape.

"I'll be in the car," I say.

I'm not going to the show. I mean, can you imagine? They're dropping me off at Andy's. We're going to "do homework" while they listen to "rock and roll." When we get there, Andy's mom makes a big fuss about their outfits.

"It's so dramatic!" she says, reaching out and lightly touching Mom's hair cliff.

"Thanks, Siobhan," says Mom. "It's more dramatic now. I forgot and had the window down for a few blocks."

"Still," says Andy's mom. She turns to Dad. "And who's this young buck?"

Andy appears behind her, just inside the door.

"Excuse me," I say, and duck past.

"What took you so long?" I say once we're inside. "I almost *died* out there!"

"Sorry," he says. "I was preparing myself. You know, mentally."

As we head for the living room we pass Andy's dad heading toward the door.

"Hi, Mr. Rossiter," I say.

"Hi-Jack!" he says. It's his standard joke for me. When he holds up both hands for the pretend hijacking, I can see that he's wearing his Kings of Country tour T-shirt. I'm pretty sure that's not a coincidence.

"Guess I'd better go be neighborly," he says, even though we're not really neighbors.

"It's not pretty," I say.

"The eighties weren't," he says.

By the time Andy and I hear my parents drive away, we're settled in at the living room table. We have our books open and look just like we would if we were doing homework. His parents duck their heads in and look just like they would if they believed us.

"We'll leave you two scholars alone," says his mom.

"Don't pull a brain muscle," says the King of Country.

Then they go upstairs, and we set up the Xbox Kinect. If you don't have one (I don't either), it's one of those video game systems that watches what you do and then has your character do the same thing in the game.

We decide to play soccer on it, so Andy takes the big square of carpet out of the closet and unrolls it right in front of the game's weird robot eyes. That way we can jump and kick without making too much noise.

We're both quiet for a second, and we can hear the TV coming through the ceiling from upstairs. It must be a dancing or singing show because first there's music, then there's applause. Those shows are pretty loud, so we figure we can have a pretty good game of soccer.

We both get carried away, but Andy's the one who brings his foot too far back on a penalty kick and clips the corner of the coffee table. We moved it back a little to put the carpet down, but I guess we didn't move it enough.

I turn around in time to see the whole table bump to a landing. Magazines shift sideways and drink coasters bounce. Right in the center of the table, a fancy-looking glass bottle wobbles twice on its little silver tray and falls over. I can see a few inches of brown liquid sloshing around inside of it.

"Nononono!" says Andy, looking over his shoulder.

He lurches back and grabs for the fancy bottle, but his body is all twisted around, and he falls and hits the table hard. Everything jumps again, higher this time. Behind him, his soccer player is basically going crazy. In front of him, the bottle skips off the edge of the table, brown liquid and all, and shatters on the floor.

"Uh-oh," he says, getting up onto his knees. His face looks shocked and pale.

We both freeze and listen. There's no sound coming from above us now, no music, and definitely no applause.

"What was that?" I whisper. "Was it, like, expensive?"

"My mom's Waterford crystal," he whispers.

"Her What-er-ferd what?" I say.

"Waterford crystal," he says. "They don't even make them anymore. Not in Ireland, anyway."

As soon as I hear the word *Ireland*, I know this is bad. Andy's mom doesn't just happen to be Irish, she's seriously *into* being Irish. She's a member of some society for it, and Andy just barely escaped Irish step-dancing lessons. Someone who would do that to her own son . . . Well, you can see how serious it is.

"What's that smell?" I say.

"Whiskey," he says. "Irish whiskey."

That's when we hear the footsteps coming down the stairs. They're coming fast. I'm actually hoping it's his dad, but it's not. Andy barely has time to get to his feet before his mom bursts into the room.

"What was th—" she starts, but she's already seen it. Her eyes are on the floor, and her jaw isn't too far away.

"My Waterford," she says.

She peels her eyes away just long enough to register the rest of the room: the soccer game on the TV and

Andy and me standing there looking as sorry as we possibly can.

"I just . . ." she says. "I don't even . . ."

And then she disappears and comes back with a roll of paper towels and a dustpan. She goes over and cleans up the mess. When she stands up again, I can see the remains of the thing in the dustpan. It broke into a few big pieces, and it seems like there should be some way to fix it. But I know there isn't.

"How?" she says, looking straight at Andy.

She looks like she's about to start crying or maybe screaming.

"I . . ." says Andy. He's in an enormous amount of trouble. "I just . . ."

"He just turned on the game," I say.

Andy looks at me. His eyes are wide open, and he's shaking his head slowly: No.

"I broke the bottle, Mrs. Rossiter," I say. "I'm very sorry about the bottle."

"It's a decanter," she says. "It was."

Her eyes slowly leave her son and land on me. They are so intense that I blink a few times and then look down.

"It was very nice," I say. "I'm sorry I broke it."

"It was very old," she says.

We're all quiet for a moment. The game makes a noise, trying to get our attention.

"Turn that off," says Andy's mom. "You won't be playing it again for a long time."

Andy walks over and turns the game off.

"Stay here," says his mom, like we have anywhere else to go. Then she leaves the room, and we hear her heading back upstairs to get his dad.

"What are you doing? Are you crazy?" Andy says in a hissy whisper. "She is going to *kill* you!"

"She can't kill me," I say. "She can only kill you!"

"OK, that's true," he says. "But you're going to get in a ton of trouble — a ton!"

"But I'll get in less than you would," I say. "It's just smarter this way."

"It's incredibly stupid!"

Now we hear them both starting down the stairs.

"Just don't say anything," I say. "We'll both get in trouble if you say something now. You for doing it, and me for saying I did it."

"I can't let you do this," he says.

His parents are almost at the bottom of the stairs, and our whispers are getting lower and lower. I try to think of some convincing way to end this.

"It was my penalty!" I say.

"What?"

"You know, the penalty kick," I say. "The one where it happened."

"So?"

"I fouled you," I say. "My fault. I got a yellow card."

"What does that even —"

And then his parents appear, and we shut up. Andy's mom gives us both a speech about taking responsibility for our actions, while his dad stands there and looks serious, sad, and sometimes a little bored.

"I'm very sorry," I say for the fourteenth time.

"Me, too," says Andy.

They keep looking at him, waiting to see if he's going to say anything else. I do, too, but he doesn't say another word until after they leave. We're sitting at the table, really doing our homework this time.

"Thanks," he says.

"Ehh," I say, waving him off. "You'd do the same for me."

And he would've. He has.

We're done with our homework by the time my parents return from the Awesome Eighties. Andy and I are both worried about what his mom is going to say to them. We're all standing there under the light on the little front porch, except for Andy's dad. He starts work early and is already in bed.

"How was he?" asks my dad. He's smiling, and his green collar is still mostly "popped."

Mrs. Rossiter looks at me. All she has to do is say a few words, and I'll be handing over my allowance to her forever. "A total hooligan," she says, but she says it like it's a joke. "As usual."

"That sounds like him, all right," says Dad with a little laugh.

"Oh, yeah?" says my mom. Her voice is more suspicious. They could be communicating on a secret mom wavelength.

"Yep," she says. "Mayhem, destruction. But it's nothing the insurance won't cover."

My mom and dad both laugh.

"Well, thanks," says my mom. "We got you this."

It's an Awesome Eighties concert T-shirt. Yeah, *that* should cover it. But amazingly, it does. I forget sometimes, our parents are friends, too.

"What do you think?" Mrs. Rossiter says to Andy, holding the shirt up in front of her.

"Dad'll love it," he says.

I thank Mrs. Rossiter again as I leave, but Andy and I don't say anything to each other. We bump fists and nod. That's what teammates do.

Chapter 7

I'm camped under a lazy fly ball in shallow left. It's totally routine, but really high. Jackson took a big cut and just got under it. It feels like I wait three minutes for it to come down, and I realize I'm nervous. Nervous for this can of corn! I don't think I've missed one of these since I was eight. That's how I know that the stakes are high.

It's the second half of practice on Tuesday, and we're having a little three-inning mini game. There's nothing unusual about that, except that our first game is Saturday. Coach is either setting the starting lineup or he already has. Obvious starters, like Manny, are playing for both teams.

I'm in left for one team, and Geoff is in left for the other. Everyone already knows one of us will start out here. When Jackson's pop-up smacks into the webbing of my glove for the third out, I cover it with my other hand. This isn't the time to take chances.

It isn't the time to pop out weakly to shallow left, either, but Jackson is safe as the starter at first. I smile a little on my way in for the top of the second inning. It has to be the first time in baseball history that someone is safe at first after popping out!

Anyway, I'm due up second, since Malfoy sat us down one, two, three in the first inning. I toss my glove to the ground, pick up the bat I like, and go straight to the on-deck circle. I take a few warm-up cuts.

It would be so sweet to get a big hit here, so sweet on so many levels. First of all, it would be off Malfoy, that smug-faced jerk-butt. Second, and a lot more important, it might give me a leg up on Geoff. He hasn't batted yet either. Coach has him batting fifth for his team, too. No one on their team has even sniffed a hit against our ace pitcher, J.P., but Geoff will get his chance in the bottom of the inning.

Dustin steps into the box. He's our catcher, and he has some pop, so he's batting cleanup. Malfoy fires in a first-pitch strike and pumps his fist as he waits to get the ball back. What a jerk: It's just one strike. I need to focus, though. In one more pitch, I could be up.

I start trying to time Malfoy's fastball. He has a pretty good one. Dustin works the count even at two balls and two strikes. On the fifth pitch, he laces one into left.

It's heading for Geoff but sinking fast. For a second, I think Geoff might run in and make some crazy diving catch, which would be great for him, or a diving miss, which would be great for me. But he does the smart thing and plays it on one hop to hold Dustin to a single.

And just like that, I'm up with a runner on. Dustin isn't fast at all, so I have to worry about hitting into a double play. As I step into the batter's box, I can see that Malfoy is really upset on the mound. It was just a single, but he's stomping around and swearing under his breath. He's the only person on the team who doesn't realize how much better a pitcher J.P. is, so he probably still thinks he has a shot at being our ace.

I go through my routine, digging my foot in, taking my four quick mini swings. Malfoy is ready before I am. As soon as my bat goes back, he fires in his best heater. That's another sign of how mad he is: The pitch is definitely faster than any of the ones to Dustin.

I take a huge cut. I mean, remember, the last time I had a bat in my hands was in a batting cage. I can still feel the sensation of all of the solid, scorched liners I'd been hitting.

Basically, I'm swinging for the fences.

I'm too late on the fastball, of course, but I hit a long foul ball well to the right of right field. I think that makes Malfoy even madder, going up there and swinging out of my shoes like that. But what can he do? He's already shown me his best heater.

He can come inside. I don't know why I didn't think of

that! The pitch cuts in toward me, chest high. It's one of those pitches where you can just tell right away you're in trouble. The ball just seems to *follow* you. I lean back as far and as fast as I can, but it isn't going to be enough. I fall backward into the dirt just as the ball hisses past me and clangs against the backstop.

That snake!

I stay down for a second to straighten out my legs and make sure everything is still in working order. The sun disappears, and I look up to see Coach standing above me. He's behind the plate as the umpire.

"You OK?" he says.

"Yep," I say, getting up. I'm not hurt, but my head is buzzing. There's something going on in my stomach, too. Butterflies, nerves, whatever you want to call it. Malfoy is a nasty dude with a nasty fastball, and man, that would've hurt. Now I have to get back in there.

"One and one," Coach calls out, squatting back down. "Watch it out there, Meacham!"

"He was crowding the plate!" Malfoy's dad shouts. That's the kind of thing you'd expect a parent to yell from the stands, not a coach from third base. Tim's dad is an assistant coach, too, but if anything, he's harder on his son. So it's not like it's impossible to be fair. And anyway, there's no way I was crowding the plate. I have my routine. I'm *always* the right distance from the plate.

I try to glare out at Malfoy, but he's already glaring in twice as hard. It's like I'd thrown at him or something. Jerk-butt.

But here's the thing: It really was a good pitch. It was a good pitch because I'm completely spooked on the next pitch and can only manage a weak hack at it. Suddenly, I'm down 1–2 and still a little shaken up.

I ask for time from Coach. He gives it to me, and I pretend there's something wrong with my shoe. When I get back into the box, I still don't feel that comfortable. I think about bunting. It's stupid to bunt with two strikes. I'm as likely to foul out as advance the runner. Plus I'm afraid Malfoy will drill me in the teeth if I square around.

I just take the next pitch. I think it's a strike, but Coach calls it a ball. It's probably punishment for the brushback pitch.

"Come on, Edgar!" Malfoy's dad yells at Coach.

"Shut up, Sam," Coach whispers behind the plate. But it's way too quiet for "Sam" to hear.

I sort of feel like I'm batting against Malfoy *and* his dad now, and I'm pretty sure Coach won't give me another charity call.

It's the fifth pitch of the at-bat, the same one Dustin lined to left. I should have the pitcher timed by now; I should be working the count. Instead, Malfoy is working me.

He drops in a slow changeup. Sneaky. After all of those fastballs, I'm about eight years ahead on the swing.

Strike three, take a seat, you suck.

We strand Dustin at third. The only good thing is that Geoff has to face J.P. in his half of the inning and goes down swinging.

"Chin music," Chester says to me as we're waiting to get picked up after practice.

"I'm tone-deaf, anyway," I say, but it's wishful thinking. I can still hear that pitch whizzing by me, clanging into the backstop. I can't quite get it out of my head.

I barely say anything on the ride home. Dad asks me if I want to get takeout from somewhere, and I just say, "Nah."

"Not even McDonald's?"

I don't say anything, and he doesn't ask again.

Chapter

8

All right, whatever. Shake it off, Jack.

I have a pretty good day in school on Wednesday. I mean, I don't humiliate myself in any major way, and it goes by quickly. Also, I talk to Katie Bowe. Kind of. I guess I'm sort of getting ahead of myself.

First period is blah, second period is bleh, and third period, well, you get the idea. But something cool happens in science class. We come in and take our seats and here comes Mr. Rommet, wearing safety goggles and some kind of heavy apron.

I don't mean the kind of apron your dad uses to cook at a barbecue with some dumb saying on it. I mean the kind you see in movies when people are messing around with uranium. Or the kind they put over you when you get X-rays at the dentist. Tim is sitting next to me, and I look over at him like, What the heck?

We all follow Rommet with our eyes as he heads up to the front of the room. That's when I notice the beaker set up on the big table. He's used it before. It's made out of that special science-class glass that you can heat up over a flame.

There's a thin metal strip in it, folded over a few times. It's like a silvery ribbon, and Mr. Rommet is carrying the sparker that he uses to light the Bunsen burner. I hear that in high school everyone gets their own Bunsen burner, and they do experiments. At Tall Pines Elementary, there is exactly one Bunsen burner, and Mr. Rommet is the only one who gets to use it. I look around at my classmates. That's probably a good call.

We know what the sparker is for, but we're wondering what he's going to light on fire with it. Meanwhile, our science teacher still hasn't said word one. He knows he has our attention in that get-up. He should have been a drama teacher.

So then he starts in: "Magnesium is a chemical element. Its symbol is Mg on the periodic table."

He points to the chart on the wall with the sparker, then continues: "It is the ninth most common substance in the universe in terms of mass." He breaks into a big smile. "And you would not beeeelieeeve how it burns! This is the stuff they use in flares."

He puts on some kind of heavy-duty glove, stands back the full length of his arm from the beaker, and starts flicking the sparker over the magnesium strip.

"Don't look directly at it!" he says, which of course makes us all look directly at it. And *FOOOOOOOF!* A spark lands, and the thing instantly turns to bright white light. It's super intense and over as soon as it begins: so, so fast.

I blink a bunch of times and then look over at Tim, just to make a "Wow" expression with my face. I can still see the exact shape of the magnesium strip in my eyes. It's sort of like a bright white half-unfolded paper clip everywhere I look. How cool is that? In a few seconds, it starts to fade away.

Anyway, it's pretty awesome. It's definitely one of Mr. Rommet's finest moments, and he knows it. He stands up there smiling and blinking.

A little while later, I'm pushing my tray along the rails in the cafeteria. I have my chocolate milk, and I'm trying to decide if I really want an apple. I close my eyes to see if I can still see the magnesium strip at all, and someone bumps my tray with theirs.

"Move it along!"

It's a girl's voice. This is a little embarrassing, but I have this feeling of — I don't know what the word is — *dread*? There's nothing worse than those mean, popular girls. I figure it's Trina or Brie or one of them. I open my eyes, exhale, and look over. It's Katie, and she's smiling.

"Thank God," I say. "I thought you were Brie."

"Are you calling me cheesy?" she says, and I laugh a little.

"Good one," I say.

"But seriously," she says, and nods toward the growing gap between me and the next kid.

"Sorry," I say, and push my tray along. I don't take an apple, and suddenly, I'm kind of nervous. It's just Katie, I tell myself, our shortstop. But I don't fool myself with that.

"That pitcher's back," she says after a few seconds.

"For Haven?" I say. "The big one?"

"That's the one," she says. "I guess he was only eleven last year!"

She says *eleven* like it's the craziest thing in the world, and it sort of is.

"No waaaaaaay!" I say. "That kid was huge. I want to see his birth certificate."

"Seriously," she says. "Maybe I'll bunt."

It occurs to me as soon as she says *bunt* that Katie already knows she's going to start, that she's going to get at least two at-bats on Saturday. Almost everyone else is sweating it out for the announcements at practice tomorrow, but this cute girl behind me in line is already thinking strategy.

I feel her bump her tray into mine. Again. I'm being a total spaz! I move my tray and try to think of something funny to say, but I'm at the front of the line now. Mrs.

Flaneau is asking me which "entrée" I want. I look down at the options. I haven't even thought about it.

"I'll have the grilled cheese and Tots while he's making up his mind," Katie says from behind me.

"See ya," she says after she gets them.

"See ya," I say. Focus, focus, focus, I tell myself. Think of something good to say. But it's too late, and I only have one thing left to focus on.

"I'll have the chicken nuggets and some Tots, please."

Chapter 9

On Thursday, I get a hit off J.P.! I know, right? Here's how it happens. Practice starts out kind of slow. Everyone is in a jumpy, weird mood because it's the last practice before our first game on Saturday.

I'd like to say that everyone is OUT FOR BLOOD because it's the last one before our first game on Saturday. That everyone is READY TO TEAR SOME CRAVEN YANKEES' HEADS OFF. But that's just not the vibe. I'm not saying that won't be the vibe on Saturday, I'm just saying there are a lot of nerves on Thursday.

Coach knows it. "I've been doing this since I was skinny," he always says. And so you look at him, and yeah, that's a lot of pounds of experience. So he eases us into things with some BP.

And so now you're thinking, Oh, you got a hit off J.P. in batting practice. But that couldn't happen because

J.P. doesn't pitch BP. That would be like using a heli-copter to go to the store. The coaches pitch, usually Wainwright. They put some on and take some off of the pitches so they can really size up our hitting and work on stuff.

It's just what I need. I'd done a pretty good job of shaking off my one at-bat in the scrimmage the other day, but I'm still kind of embarrassed about it. I got owned by Malfoy, basically. Not because he's that great a pitcher. I mean, he's good, but I've gotten hits off him before. It was because I got scared, and that's embarrassing. I hate both those feelings: being afraid and being embarrassed.

But Coach isn't going to hit me. I take my time and go through my full routine at the plate, digging in, taking my mini swings, and all that.

"All right, Garciaparra," he says. I know who that is. A long time ago, Nomar Garciaparra was a big star for the Red Sox. I figure he took a really long time at the plate. Anyway, I cock my bat back and I'm ready to go.

Maybe Coach is going easy on me, taking a little off rather than putting a little on. He was behind the plate when I got knocked off it, and he had a front row seat when I gave up on that at-bat. Whatever the case, I'm really drilling the ball.

"Who died and made you a hitter?" says Dustin, hang-ing on the wire backstop and waiting his turn.

I step into another one and hit it hard to left.

"I don't know, but we should check the obituaries," I say. "Must've been someone good."

"SHUHH!" says Dustin. "Someone lucky."

I said before that the outfield gets really crowded during BP. I probably don't have to worry about Geoff making a great catch on one of the bombs I'm hitting, but I don't want to chance it. I start moving the ball around. I hit some sharp grounders and a few shots to right (you just wait on the ball a little longer). I even square around to bunt once. Coach likes it when we "work on the fundamentals," but everyone in the outfield boos.

I wave them off and leave the plate feeling pretty good about my swing, pretty darn good. Then I pick up my glove and hustle out to left field.

We do some fielding drills, the lawsuit drill again, and then it's the pitchers' turn. I mean, in Little League, half the team will pitch at some point. But we all know this is about getting our big guns game-ready. That means J.P. and Malfoy and Dustin, who has the third-best arm.

Coach wants them to face live hitting. I'm the second guy up against J.P., after Jackson goes down swinging. Maybe Coach just doesn't want me facing Malfoy again right away, but I decide it's because I lit it up in BP.

"Kass, shift over there to left," Coach calls to Geoff as I pick up a bat. I don't like that, but I tell myself it's only because I'm hitting. It's normal defense in the field, and Assistant Coach Liu is the umpire.

Anyway, I dig in, but I don't take as long this time. Then I look out at the beast on the mound. J.P. is kind of a big dude, but not that big. He's just really good.

I don't know if you've ever watched the Little League World Series, but you know how most of those teams have one kid who's just, like, a monster? You know, maybe he's a little bigger than the other kids and actually has some breaking stuff? Maybe he'll take on, like, the team from the Netherlands and strike out thirteen out of eighteen? Well, that's J.P.

I don't think he's ever struck out quite that many, but he's been close. I think he got ten once last season, and that was his first year in majors. The fact that this town isn't going anywhere near the Little League World Series isn't his fault. He made the All-Star team last year, easy. There just aren't enough kids like him around here.

Anyway, that's who I'm staring out at. And he isn't glaring back at me, like Malfoy does. J.P. is just looking in for the sign. If he looks anything, it's maybe just a little bored.

It's the same way in school. Everyone likes him because he's so good, but you can never really tell if he likes you, too. He's like a rock star. Mostly he hangs out with Manny, another guy everyone likes. He just seems a little above it all. And anyway, he probably gets tired of striking out the same kids in practice.

But here's the thing: He doesn't strike me out. I take the first pitch. I'm hoping to get ahead in the count and maybe work a walk, but he paints the outside edge of the plate for strike one.

Now I have to take the bat off my shoulder. I just get a hunch. He'd gone outside on the first pitch, and I figure he might come inside on the next one. Because, I mean, this is still just practice. He's facing "live hitting," and I'm facing "live pitching," but it's still just practice at Culbreath Field, just like every other Tuesday and Thursday. He'll want to work both sides of the plate.

So I figure: heater inside. I start swinging at it almost before it leaves his hand. You sort of have to do that with J.P., and of course you look like a total idiot if it's anything off-speed, but it isn't. I guess inside fastball, and that's what he throws. It comes in just a little above the knees, and I have it timed.

I hear the *ping* of the aluminum and feel the sting in my hands. I sprint down to first base and make it easily.

"Well, well, well!" says Coach. "Let's try that again."

I groan and head back in. I know how lucky I got, and when I look out at the mound this time, J.P. doesn't seem bored anymore. Not even a little bit.

He strikes me out on three pitches. He has his choice of weapons on the third pitch, and he goes with the changeup. Remember how I said you could look like a real idiot on those? Yeah, well I prove it big-time on that swing.

Coach calls Chester in to hit.

We bump fists as we pass.

"Sweet hit," he says. "Killed it."

"Thanks. Nice day for a walk," I say, because everyone and his brother knows Chester is heading in to test J.P.'s control with that tiny strike zone of his.

Geoff is still in left, so there's no place for me in the field. I go over to sit in the grass with the others, and I get some high fives.

"You're on fire today," says Evan, a really good fifth grader who's battling Tim for the start at second. "I'd kill for a solid hit off J.P."

"Thanks, man," I say. "Think I just used up my lifetime supply."

"Good day for it," he says. "Really good."

All I can do is agree. I just got a hit off John Piersol "J.P." Walters. And I did it on the day Coach is going to name the opening day starters.

Chapter 10

Maybe it seems like I'm making a big deal out of starting. It's Little League, so everyone is going to get at least one at-bat and some time in the field anyway. But our roster is maxed out, and that's a lot of kids to stuff into a six-inning game. And it's not like the big leagues, because starters can come back in the game after they're subbed for.

If you're a starter on my team, you're going to be in there at the beginning, and at the end, too, if it's close. Because you're the best one at your position, and who doesn't want that? My friends and I have played ball for most of our lives, and this is our last year of Little League. We don't want to watch it from the bench.

So when Coach lines us up at the end of practice on Thursday, my stomach is turning over on itself, and my heart is beating like it's trying to break out of my chest.

Am I going to be scrambling to get my first at-bat as a sub in the fourth inning, or am I going to be digging in, nice and easy, in the first or second?

And of course, Coach makes us wait. He's been using this one thing, this one little word to make us bust our butts. He's made everyone think they have a shot. So I guess he feels like he has to announce it in some special way. What he does is line us up on the field.

You know how every position has a number when you're scoring the game, like pitcher is number one? He goes in that order, scorecard order. Left field isn't until number seven.

So we're standing there, all in a line in front of the bleachers. It's kind of a gray day. Right before Coach starts talking, a big gust of wind blows in from the side, and we all grab our caps so they don't blow off.

I take a breath and nod over at Geoff. We have a long wait, and it's like no hard feelings, either way. He nods back. I like Geoff, it's just that he's the competition.

"One!" says Coach. We don't really need to wait for him to call out J.P.'s name, but we all do anyway. Even J.P. stands there like he's waiting in line at the caf, like he has no idea anything is going to happen.

"Get out there, Walters," Wainwright says.

J.P. jogs out to the mound, nice and easy, like it's for a fielding drill or something. Man, to be that good, just for one day . . . A few spots down, Malfoy deflates. The look on his face is somewhere between disappointment and stomach pain. He really thought he had a shot. I can't blame him for wanting it. He's been playing as long as I have. This year means the same thing to him.

"Two," Coach says. "You know the spot, Cuddy."

Not much drama there, either. Good catchers are as rare as plutonium in Little League. Dustin sprints over and stands behind the plate.

"Three, Jackson," says Coach, and Jackson makes the short trip to first base. No surprises so far, but there's no clear front-runner for the next spot. One kid will be surprised, and one kid will be disappointed.

"Four," says Coach, and I elbow Andy in the side.

"Let's go, Timmaaaay!" he says under his breath.

"Liu," says Coach. "Get out there."

"Yessss!" Andy and I whisper.

One of the younger kids gives us a look, but we don't care. We low-five. This is no offense to Evan, not at all, but he's still got another year, and Timmy's our friend.

"Five," says Coach.

I hear Andy take a quick, sharp breath next to me. I hold my breath, too.

"Don't make me look bad, Rossiter," Coach says.

Sweeeeeeeeeeeeeet!

Andy jogs out to third without looking back. It's rude to look back: You might see the guy you beat out. That's Chester, but he's a good sport about it. He just doesn't have a big enough arm for that long throw across the diamond. (Of course, nothing about Chester is all that big.) He's going to end up second string at both spots on the left side of the infield, because he won't beat out Katie at short, either. He'll still get plenty of playing time and at-bats, though. He's our supersub.

I don't hear Coach call Katie's name, because right about then, my heart climbs into my head and starts pounding there, too. One more until left field.

I see Katie jog out to short, her ponytail flicking left-right, left-right.

B-dum! B-dum! B-dum! My heart is pounding so hard I wonder if I'll even hear Coach announce it.

"Seven," he says.

B-DUM! B-DUM! B-DUM!

"Mogens."

That's me. That's me!

Chapter

11

Yes! Yeeeeessssss!

SWEEEEEEEEEEEEEEEEEEEEEEEEEEEEEEEEEE-
EEETTTTTTTTTTT!!!!!

I just stand out there in left, feeling my heart settle back into my chest and go back to its day job. I look around: It's the nicest windy gray day I've ever seen.

Manny gets the start in center for the second straight year, and Malfoy is over in right. They put him over there because not much gets hit that way, so it's easy to sub in for him if he needs to come in to pitch. It's where they put J.P. when he doesn't start, too.

The main thing is that Malfoy is in right. Good, I think. Stay over there. He's a pain when he's in center, always trying to call you off so he can come all the way over and snag a high pop-up.

After a while, Coach calls us back in and says: "That's the starting lineup for Saturday. Nothing is set in stone after that. You got me? You want to stay there, you've got to earn it. You other guys want to grab one of those spots, you've got to earn that, too."

He pauses, then says, "I don't want a repeat of last year."

The Craven Yankees beat us after we blew a late lead last year. Most of us were on the team for that, and the new kids have at least heard about it. The Craven Yankees' coach is a loud, angry jerk, and the team is pretty much the same way. No one wants to lose to them again.

Coach draws a line in the dirt of the first-base line with the toe of his shoe. We all look at it, and he erases it with his other foot.

"That's how quick it could go," he says. "You got me?"

"Yes, Coach!" we yell.

It's still sweet.

Chapter

12

Friday night: big whoop-de-doo!

There are all of those songs and stuff about Friday night, but there's not much to it when you're twelve. I guess the big thing is that there's no school for two days, so you don't have to do any homework. I usually start mine on Saturday, just so I won't have to spend all Sunday doing it. No homework is good, but I don't think anyone has ever written a song about it.

All I've got planned for tonight is watching the baseball game with Mom and Dad. Yeah, rock on, right?

I don't mind, though. I kind of like it. I've been thinking about the game against Haven all day, and there aren't a lot of things that can get my mind off that. Definitely not school. But it's funny: Sometimes the best way to distract yourself from baseball is with baseball.

It's some special game in Japan, and it's Dodgers versus Brewers. It's like they set out to scientifically select the two teams I know the least about. It seems kind of random, like there was this big meeting of all thirty teams, and the Dodgers and Brewers were just the last two to say, "Not it!"

It's OK. Both teams have some good players, and we have chips and salsa and soda and some ice cream for later. It will be time for bed when it's over, and when I get up, it will be game day.

Sometimes I sit between Mom and Dad for games, and sometimes they sit next to each other and I sit on one side. Sometimes it's like I can sort of tell how things are going between them by where I wind up sitting.

Tonight, they're over on the left side of the couch and I'm on the right. That's good: They're probably still in one of their lovey-dovey phases after that concert, and I don't really like to sit between them anymore. I'm not eight, you know?

The second batter goes deep for Milwaukee. "One-nothing, Brew Crew!" says the announcer.

I settle into stuffing my face and watching the game. I like to watch the left fielders when no one else is paying attention to them, like when the runner is taking a lead off second. What would it be like to play in the big leagues? What would it be like to watch that guy take that lead from a hundred feet away? Awesome, right? It would be awesome.

The Dodgers get last licks in the inning, so I ask, "How do they decide who's the home team when they're both in Japan?"

"Coin toss?" says Mom.

"Rock-paper-samurai swords?" says Dad.

Ugh.

"That was pretty bad, hon," says Mom.

"Yeah, like even worse than usual," I say.

"What are you, teaming up on me now?" says Dad, which gives us an idea.

Just to make it more interesting, we choose sides. We don't have any samurai swords, so we toss a coin to see who picks. Dad wins the toss and chooses the Brewers. He won't say whether it's because they've got the lead or because he's got a beer. Mom and I, the soda swiggers, end up rooting for the Dodgers.

Mom knows baseball. On TV, the mom is always in the other room when the dad is watching baseball with his buddies; you know, rolling her eyes when they spill nachos on the carpet. In real life, Mom has a Diet Coke and a seat on the couch.

She knows plenty about the game. I don't know if she always has, but she's been taking me to practices and games since T-ball. She's been cheering from the stands and listening to me complain and brag and everything in between for years. These days, she can tell you which team in the NL Central has the best double-play combo.

The two of us piece together what we know about the Dodgers and combine into a halfway decent L.A. fan.

"This guy's pretty good," I say. "That guy used to be with the Tigers."

"He put a good swing on that one," Mom says.

In the fifth she says, "I wonder if they'll pinch-hit for the pitcher?"

"Yeah," I say, "he doesn't have it tonight."

And he doesn't, so we have to listen to Dad's Brewer trash talk. If you didn't know better, you'd think he'd been a fan his whole life. Of course, he has it easy, since he can just do play-by-play on their home runs and stolen bases. It's like the Dodger pitcher and catcher both got their arms secondhand.

The L.A. bullpen is better, though. (And they do pinch-hit for the starter in the fifth.) The Dodgers mount a little comeback in the seventh. It's just a few runs, but it's enough to keep us from flipping the channel. By that point, Mom and I are calling them Los Dodgeros for no good reason, and it's like *we* have been fans our whole lives.

It isn't even a save opportunity, but the Brewers bring in their closer and he lights-outs my poor Dodgeros. After that, I boo Dad one more time and head to my room. He makes a motorboat sound with his lips and waves me away. He's on his fifth beer, at least, and is in a really good mood.

Up in my room, I think about the game. I don't mean Dodgers-Brewers. I mean mine.

Chapter 13

We arrive at the game early, but it seems like everyone on the team does. First game of the season! Some of us are milling around and talking to each other. Others are still sitting in their parents' cars because it's a cold morning.

I'm talking to Andy, and we're both stomping the ground and blowing into our hands. The Weather Channel said it was forty-eight just before I left home. The air is kind of damp, too, which makes it feel colder. I'd play baseball on the Siberian tundra, but to be honest, I like it warmer. Everyone does.

Everything stings more when it's cold: The bat stings your hands when you make bad contact, and the ball stings more when you catch it on the palm. It would definitely sting more if you got beaned.

Most of us are wearing long-sleeved T-shirts under our jerseys. That's not much in terms of warmth, but it's sort of uncool to wear anything heavier. Plus, it's still early. First pitch is a ways away, and it will probably warm up some by then. The cloud cover could burn off, and next thing you know you're standing around sweating.

Anyway, we all hope we'll be circling the bases and making so many great plays in the field that we can just stay warm that way. A few of the younger kids have sweatshirts on under their jerseys, but you can't really blame them. As far as I'm concerned, the coldest place on the entire planet is sitting on the bench.

After fifteen minutes, the last few Braves arrive, and the others finally climb out of their cars. They look up at the gray sky like it just punched them. So here we are: the Tall Pines Braves, all present and accounted for. And there still isn't a single Craven Yankee in sight, just some unfamiliar parents sitting together on the bleachers. It was the same thing last year. I think the Yankees make a point of arriving late. It's like psychological warfare or something: build up the suspense.

Normally I'd say it just gives them less time to warm up. Today, I think it gives them less time to cool down. Whatever the case, we take the field to stretch and run through some drills. With only one team here, it could almost be a practice. If they don't arrive soon, it will be.

We have league umps for games, and they stand together sipping coffee. I guess it's coffee, anyway, because they hold their hands around the cups like they're warm rocks. Dad let me try coffee once when I was seven. I don't know how anyone ever drinks that stuff.

Anyway, we're just running through the normal pre-game stuff, and here comes this big, shiny passenger van, pulling in to the lot and honking its horn. It's dark blue, Yankees blue. They must have rented it for game day.

"You've got to be kidding me," I say.

As soon as it pulls to a stop, the side door slides open, and the Haven Yankees start pouring out of it like it's a landing craft in a World War II movie.

"Hey, Jack," Dustin says.

"Yeah?"

"What's dark blue and full of idiots?"

I laugh and throw the ball back to him.

The Haven coach heads right for Coach Wainwright. He starts barking words at Coach when he's still ten feet away. I notice the two of them don't shake hands, and I sort of understand why the Haven games always seem to mean a little more to Coach than the others.

Anyway, long story short, they kick us off the field. They're late (and whose fault is that?), so they need to warm up right away. We're almost done, anyway, but it's still annoying.

I'm glad when the officials tell them to hurry it up. Now that their coffee cups are cold and empty, they want to get the game started. Fine with us, we were on time.

The Haven coach barks about that, too: yap, yap, yap. Finally, he says, "All right, give us ten minutes."

"You got ten," says the home plate ump.

Ten minutes till the start of the season. I can't wait!

Chapter 14

We're in the field to start things off. I wave to Mom and Dad once — just once, I swear — and then look in toward the plate. J.P. is finishing up his warm-up throws. He's just getting going, but I can hear the ball hitting the mitt clearly all the way in left. I wonder what it sounds like to the kids on the Haven bench.

They'd all know his name, of course. Walters, they'd be saying. That's J.P. Walters. The new kids on the team would be trying not to stare. It's true what they say: A really good pitcher, a real ace, has a strike on the hitters before they even step to the plate.

Anyway, we're the home team. It's kind of funny because this isn't our home field. It isn't where we practice, anyway. Culbreath Field is kind of a dump when it comes right down to it. "Not suitable for entertaining," Coach always says.

It's sort of a disappointment because it's a dump, but it's our dump. It would be nice to play on the same field you practice on. As it is, it's sort of like an away game for us, too.

Pop! I hear J.P.'s last warm-up toss. That makes me feel at home, at least.

"Look alive!" Coach shouts out to us. Then he gets Malfoy's attention and waves him a little deeper back. Their first batter is a lefty, so he's more likely to hit it to right. But he strikes out on four pitches, all fastballs. Lefty-righty matchups don't mean much to J.P.

Their second batter draws a walk, though. You can see J.P. doesn't like a few of the calls. Maybe he's a little shaken up or afraid the umpire is "squeezing the strike zone" on him. They did that a lot last year, too, just because he's so good.

Anyway, he grooves the first pitch to the next batter right down the middle, looking for strike one. This is their number three hitter, so one of their best. He puts a good swing on it and hits a hot shot to Andy at third. Andy tries to field it on one hop, but it kind of eats him up and he doesn't field it cleanly. By the time he gets it, he has to make a really strong throw just to get the runner at first.

So, there are two outs, but there's a runner in scoring position at second.

Their cleanup hitter is up next. It's their big pitcher.

He's first-pitch swinging, looking for another one in the center of the plate. But J.P. is smart and throws a fastball up in the zone.

The kid, his name is Tebow, gets underneath it and hits a high pop-up in my direction. I try to get a bead on it, but it keeps carrying. I start backpedaling underneath it, slowly at first and then faster.

I start thinking about the fence, somewhere behind me but coming up fast. I can't turn around to see, or I'll lose track of the ball. If I hit the fence, I hit the fence, I tell myself. But my brain can't quite let it go. I'm backpedaling fast, and hitting the fence would be a train wreck.

The ball is coming down now. There's no sound at a moment like that, just your eyes, your glove, and the ball. Three more quick steps back, and it slaps into my glove for out number three.

"There ya go, Mogens!" someone calls.

I look in and realize it's Geoff. Kind of a classy move, right?

Before I jog in to our bench, I turn around to check. The fence is maybe three feet behind me. This field is nice, but it needs a warning track. Andy waits for me at third, and we jog in together.

"Nice throw," I say.

"Nice catch," he says, and slaps me on the arm with his glove.

"Man," I say, "that big dude was fooled on the pitch and almost hit it out!"

"Yeah," says Andy. "Serious power. And now we have to try to get a hit off him."

"Great," I say. "Just great."

Chapter 15

I'm up fifth and don't really think I'll get to the plate in the first inning against that big ol' horse they have pitching. I figure maybe someone will get on base ahead of me, and I'll end up leading off the second.

Turns out Tebow is kind of wild today. He walks Manny and then strikes out Andy on a full count. Andy kind of gets overpowered by a fastball on strike three and rolls his eyes at me on the way back to the bench.

"Good cut!" I say to him when he gets back. "Way to stay aggressive."

"Should've taken it," he says.

"Yeah," I admit. "Looked high."

Andy looks back over his shoulder at the pitcher. "This guy's all over the place today. I did him a favor swinging."

"Yeah," I say. "Still a good cut."

Andy sits down and I do some stretches to loosen up. I think about what he said: "all over the place." It seems like such a good thing.

Tebow grooves one to Jackson, trying to get ahead in the count, just like J.P. had grooved one to Tebow. But Jackson doesn't miss. He slaps a single into shallow left, and just like that, we have runners on first and third with one out.

Dustin is batting cleanup. I watch his at-bat from the on-deck circle. Unless he hits into a double play, I'll be up this inning. And unless he hits a homer, I'll be up with runners on.

I take some practice swings and try to time Tebow's pitches. Dustin takes a strike and then swings through one. Pitch number three is in the dirt. Their catcher makes a good play to keep it in front of him and maybe save a run. All three pitches are really fast.

Dustin swings through the next one to strike out, and it seems like maybe Tebow is settling down. I take a deep breath and head to the plate with two out and two on. Runners on base: ducks on the pond . . . I always liked that saying.

I'm a little nervous, sure. But I'm also sort of comfortable. I've done this so many times before: batting cages, batting practice, and game after game, all the way up the

Little League ladder. This guy is really bringing it, I know that, and maybe he's a little wild. J.P. is on deck, and Katie is in the hole, and it's my job to keep the inning going.

I step to the plate like I always do, and I go through my routine. I'm not sure how much time the ump will give me, so I get right to it.

First, I sort of dig my front foot in. I twist the toes into the dirt at the front of the batter's box a few times. Then I settle my weight onto my back foot.

The ump still hasn't said anything, so I begin my mini swings: two fast and two slow.

"All right," the ump says behind me, but I'm already done.

I cock my bat back and look up. I squint out at the mound. Tebow goes into his windup and my eyes are laser-focused. I need to pick up the ball as soon as it leaves his hand.

His arm comes up and forward, and the ball is out and headed toward the plate. But something is wrong. The pitch is high and bearing in. I should just take this one, get ahead in the count, ball one, but it just keeps bearing in on me. It's a fastball, and suddenly I know: I'm going to get hit. I'm going to get hit in the head.

All I have time to do is flinch. And then it's like an explosion, so much sound and power. It's like when a thunderstorm is right on top of you, when the lightning and the thunder come at the same time. I'm knocked off my feet at the same instant I hear the crack.

I think it hit my helmet, right on the earpiece, but I don't know anything for sure. That crack could have been my skull. All I know is that I'm on the ground, looking up. Their catcher is standing over me, looking down, and then the ump is, too, and then more people. Everything looks twisted and fractured, and that's how I realize there are tears in my eyes.

I honestly don't realize how bad it is until I see Coach. He says a lot of things, but the words I hear are these:

"Pinch-runner."

Part II
IN THE DIRT

Chapter 16

There's something I would like to say, like, officially: Oooooooooowwwww!

I'm lying there at home plate, looking up at all the people standing over me in a circle. Their catcher has his mask pushed up on top of his head. The ump's mask is totally off, and he has this weird look on his face, like he's about to start laughing or crying. Then there's Coach and someone I don't know. And they're all still talking. I know it's about me, but I'm not catching most of it.

I'm looking up at the sky, and it feels like the whole world is vibrating. I have that feeling you get after you drop something, like you need to bend down and pick it up. Except I'm already down, and the thing I want to pick up might be my head.

They take turns kneeling down and asking me things. Coach leans close and says, "You all right there, Mogens?"

"I got hit!" I say.

Like he wouldn't know that. I really need to shake this off. I wipe my arm across my face then turn my head to the left and spot my batting helmet lying on the ground. That's what I wanted to pick up.

"I get to go to first base," I say.

I try to get up, but Coach puts his hand on my shoulder. That sort of annoys me. I want to get up now: pinch-runner, my big red monkey-butt!

Coach turns and says something to Dustin. And then I see the others, in a semicircle just outside the first group. There's Andy, Jackson, and the big pitcher who hit me, Tebow. Jackson sort of shoulders past him, maybe rougher than he needs to, but the pitcher doesn't seem to notice.

Someone asks me if I can get up. "I'm trying!" I say. "Coach won't let me!"

But then it occurs to me that it might have been Coach who asked, and what he means is should I.

And then I can hear my mom coming from about twenty feet away. She's saying, "Let me through," and "That's my son," and her voice is louder and higher than the others, like a siren. All I can do is pray she doesn't call me sugar bear or honey bunchkin or any of those other things she does sometimes at home. Oh, man: I bet she will.

Finally, she and Dad make it through the other parents. Once they arrive, everyone else relaxes a little. Not that it changes anything, but it sort of lets the others off the hook a little. It sort of makes me think of the lawsuit drill.

Anyway, Coach takes his hand away, and I get up without too much trouble. Mom tries to help, but I hurry so I can do it on my own. I look at her, trying to make my eyes say: "no honey bunchkin." Luckily, she's too busy asking me questions to say anything else.

They start walking me over to the bleachers. I don't want to come out of the game, but I guess I don't have a choice. This thought pops into my head: Little League is like a magic spell. It's kids only, like Peter Pan or something, and once a parent touches you, it's over. The spell is broken. I guess that's a weird thought, but whatever: I was just drilled in the *cranium*. I'm just glad my brain is still in the thought-producing business.

I head toward the gap in the fence that leads to the bleachers, but I sort of drag my feet a little to let them know I'm not happy about it. And then I sit there. I try to watch the game and not listen to what people are saying around me, but the game still hasn't started again. That seems weird, too.

Dad leaves and comes back with an ice pack. It's one of those chemical ones, where you just twist it and snap open some pouch inside and it gets really cold. So then, of course, coldest day in weeks, and they put the thing right on my head.

"Can you hold this here?" Dad says, pushing the thing into the left side of my head.

"Of course!" I say, because I'd just been insisting that I should still be in the game.

I ask for my glove, and Dad looks at me suspiciously.

"What? I'm not going to run out onto the field!" I say. We're still up to bat, anyway. "What am I gonna do, field for the other team?"

So someone gets my glove, some adult, because the players are finally getting back to business. Jackson is back on base waiting around for the pitching change. They just lifted that pitcher, Tebow.

I look around the field, trying to find him and wondering why the game hasn't started yet. And then I realize that he's coming right toward me. I can feel the people around me tense up. I hear some old guy suck in his breath. I watch Tebow step up onto the first row of the bleachers. I think maybe I'm supposed to fight him, but I really don't want anything else hitting my head right now, just when it's starting to get numb.

"Sorry," he says, holding out one big hand.

"No problem," I say.

I raise the hand that's not holding the ice pack, and we shake.

"Didn't have it today," he says.

"Yeah, I could see you were kind of wild," I say. "Thought maybe you were settling down."

It feels a little weird to talk, but it doesn't really hurt that much.

"Yeah," he says, "so did I!"

He sort of grimaces at that last part. Then he turns around and heads back down the bleachers.

He's an OK kid, that Tebow, even if he just drilled me in the head with a rock-hard missile.

Someone hands me my glove, and I put it on so that I can hold the ice pack with it. That way my hand won't be so cold while I'm freezing my brain.

Finally, the game is starting up again. The Haven coach shuffles some players and sticks Tebow in the outfield, where he can't do any more damage. I guess the umps had just given him, like, extended time-out to come over and make nice.

And what was Jackson doing at home plate, now that I think about it? My thinking is clearing up. Suddenly, I'm sort of annoyed that they're bending the rules around so much.

My head is getting really cold, like so-cold-it-hurts cold, and not just the surface, either. And I'm no doctor, but are you really supposed to do that to your brain?

"Is this a good idea?" I say. I don't say it to Mom or Dad in particular, but they're both hovering around me so they both hear. And just like that they start walking me over to the car. They're on both sides of me, and they each have an elbow. I try to shake them off, but they're holding on so tight it's like they're going to make a wish.

Geoff is on first base, even though that should be my base. J.P. is just stepping to the plate. I think I might get to see a swing or two. He has power, but he kind of strikes out a lot. Everyone starts clapping for some reason, and he steps back out of the box.

It seems so dumb. Yeah, he's a great pitcher, but he hasn't even taken a swing, so why are they all clapping for him? And then I realize they're clapping for me. That seems dumb, too. What did I do except get hit in the head? Yeah, what a skill . . . I hold up my hand because I don't want to be rude, and they clap louder. It's still dumb, but I admit that I kind of smile.

And then we're at the car and Mom is closing the door for me. I get shotgun without even calling it. All of a sudden, Dad is in a huge hurry and driving about a hundred miles per hour. His eyes stay on the road this time.

I don't have to wait long for the doctor. It's not like there are a lot of drive-by shootings to attend to out here in the sticks.

"So we meet again," says Dr. Redick.

I have to smile at that. I've been here before, for my ankle and my wrist and my other ankle. Dr. Redick is probably the leading expert on which kids around here play sports and which ones don't.

"Yeah," I say.

"I see you've stepped it up this time," he says.

"Yeah," I say, "I thought you might be getting bored of ankles."

He takes the ice pack and throws it away. He doesn't ask about it or say that it was the right or wrong thing to do, he just takes it from me like it's a leaf that I didn't realize I had in my hair.

Then he asks me some questions and makes me follow a light with my eyes.

"Is there a ringing in your ears?" he asks. "Anything like that?"

I try to listen to the inside of my head, which is weird. "Maybe, like, a hum?" I say. "A humming, maybe?"

"A humming?" he says.

He flicks his eyes up toward the ceiling.

I look up at the big bank of lights there. I listen again, and yep, that's what that is. "Oh," I say.

That's kind of embarrassing. Duh. He asks me some more questions and pushes my hair aside to take a look at the knot I can feel just above my left ear. The skin feels really tight, and it hurts when he touches it.

"Maybe a minor concussion," he says when he's done. "Maybe not. Nothing too serious, but I wouldn't run out and get another one anytime soon."

It's not clear if he's talking to me or my parents, but I look him in the eye because it's my head.

"Does it hurt now?" he asks, and now he's talking to me.

"Yeah," I say, "a little."

And it does, but it's just a normal sort of hurt, as if I got punched. It isn't some special brain pain or anything.

"It's what we used to call getting your bell rung when I was a kid," he says.

Adults are always saying things like that: "When I was a kid . . ." Like life was so much tougher and more hardcore back then. I sort of want to say something like, Yeah, what happened? Did the first caveman wheel run over your head?

I don't, though. I like Dr. Redick. And anyway, I figure I'll be back again before too long.

"I got my bell rung," I say. I guess I'm sort of trying it out to see how it will sound in school on Monday. Pretty good. You know: tough. "I got my bell rung; no biggie. . . ."

After I get out of the little white room, my mom lets me borrow her cell phone. I don't bring mine to games: no pockets. The game must be over by now, so I call Andy to get the scoop. He picks up right away and says, "Hey, my man. How *are* you?"

I hold the phone against my right ear, because of that knot above my left.

"OK," I say.

"We won," he says. "Seven-zip."

94

"Sweet," I say. "Did I score?"

What I mean is, Did Geoff come around to score when he was pinch-running for me? And with anyone other than Andy, that's probably what I'd have to say. But Andy knows what I mean, just like he always does.

"Nah," he says. He pauses, setting something up.

"Yeah?"

"Thrown out at the plate!" he blurts.

"No way!" I say.

I wince because shouting into the phone hurts my head, but it's not too bad, and I don't miss anything. "Yuh-huh," he says. "Gunned down!"

I pause to make sure I'm OK, which is fine because it gives me time to think of something good. "Of course, you know: I woulda made it."

"Oh, by a mile. No doubt."

Andy laughs and so do I, even though that doesn't feel so great, either. Mostly, I'm just glad we won.

People look over at me. A kid sitting there in the hospital lobby, laughing into a cell phone while his mom signs some forms up at the desk. They probably think it's "insensitive" or whatever. I don't see it that way: I'm injured. Totally legit. I have as much reason to be here as any of the people looking over at me.

But I'm leaving now. The sooner Mom can sign her name, like, seventeen times, the sooner we'll be out of here. Dad has already gone to get the car.

"J.P. was really mad after you got hit," Andy is saying. "They just had no shot at him after that. If it was possible to score less than zero, they would have."

I feel good about that, like I contributed. Mom finishes the last form and pushes it across the desk to the lady. I say bye to Andy and hand the phone back to her.

"Got everything?" she says.

"Except for the pieces I left on the field," I say.

She doesn't think that's funny.

Chapter 17

We pull into the driveway. It sort of catches me by surprise that we're home already. I'm thinking about one of things Dr. Redick said: "No structural damage." That just seems so funny to me because the "structure" he's talking about is my head!

By now, Mom and Dad have figured out that it's mostly good news and are in a much better mood.

"It never really worked right in the first place," Dad says to Mom in the front seat, still talking about my head.

"Nothing to be done at this point," Mom says. "Maybe we should think about boarding school."

Yeah, ha-ha-ha. Everyone is having fun now. I want to say, Hey! I got hit in the head here. But they're just relieved. I can hear it in their voices. They'd been insanely tense, like seriously crazy, on the drive to the hospital.

"Home again, home again," Dad says as the car comes to a stop.

Jiggedy jog, I think, because that's the rest of it.

I get out and start up the walkway. I look at our yellow house, not big but not little. I look up at my bedroom window on the second floor. It feels like I've been away for a long time because so much has happened since I left.

I try to remember what games are on TV today and what snacks we have in the kitchen. Chips definitely, but I don't know if we have any dip left. Then Nax appears in the window of the front door, barking and going crazy.

"Someone needs to be walked," Mom says behind me. Normally, that would be my cue, but today she says, "I'll take him."

"Nah," I say. "I'm fine."

The TV can wait.

"Do you want to eat before or after?" Mom says once we're inside.

"After," I say, because I already have the leash out, and Nax goes into hyperdrive when that happens.

He bursts through the front door like a horse busts out of the gate at the Kentucky Derby. He doesn't really settle down until we get to the Rail Trail behind our house. Then he comes up and rubs the gunk in the corner of his eye off against my pant leg and licks my hand.

"Hey, boy," I say.

A bicyclist comes whizzing by, and I have to hold Nax back so he won't cause an accident. Then it's just the two of us for a while. The day still isn't that warm, so I grabbed my favorite sweatshirt before I left. It was so big for me when I got it on vacation a few years ago, but now it fits perfectly and has been softened up by a hundred washes.

"Little chilly, huh?" I say, because, yeah, sometimes I talk to my dog. It's not that I think he can understand all the words, but he can understand some words, like *walk*. And he can definitely tell when I'm happy or upset or whatever.

He looks back at me and then lets out one small bark, almost like a whoop. See? It's like he agrees. His eyes are all over the trail, looking for squirrels.

"I got hit in the head, boy," I say. "It hurt."

It would be funny if he said *ruff*. He really does say that sometimes, but he doesn't say anything now. He just looks back at me again. His eyes are big and wet and blank, so I go on.

"I guess it was dumb. I mean, the pitcher had zero control, and I didn't even really think about that. . . ."

But Nax isn't listening anymore. He hasn't seen a squirrel yet, and he's getting antsy, pulling harder on the leash.

"Until I got hit," I say, wrapping it up.

I touch the side of my head. It's a little sore and a little swollen, just in that one spot. *Tender*, that's the word. It feels a little tender.

Thank God for batting helmets. What if I hadn't been wearing one? I picture the ball bearing in on me. No, not picture: I remember. I remember the ball coming straight for me, and I have to shake the thought out of my tender, stupid head. I need to forget about that.

Nax jerks on his leash, and I snap back to reality. "All right," I say. "Let's find you a squirrel."

Nax jumps at the end of his leash. *Squirrel* is another word he knows.

"A fat gray squirrel," I say, and he spins around in excitement.

Then he squats and takes a dump, so he can move faster, I guess. He doesn't move off the paved part of the Rail Trail this time, so I reach into my pocket for the Baggie.

Chapter 18

It's Saturday night: time to start my homework. I'm up in my room, pushing around the pile of books and notebooks I dumped out onto my bed.

Then I make individual piles. I put my notebook for English on the bottom of one pile, put the textbook on top, and then the little paperback copy of *The Island of Dr. Moreau* on top of that. The whole thing forms a little pyramid. Doing this does not help me get my homework done at all, in any way.

I'm just putting it off. What's the word, *procrastinating*? And see, right there, I think I should get credit for that, like vocabulary credit. And maybe something for the pyramid. Isn't there a class called geometry, in high school, maybe? I should get advanced placement credit!

And then I have another thought: Maybe I won't have to do homework this weekend. After all, I got hit in the head. Apart from the batting helmet and my skull, I got *hit in the brain*. How could they ask a kid who had practically been hit in the brain to do homework so soon?

Maybe I can't even read right now, I think. But then I realize I've been reading the sports ticker at the bottom of the screen on ESPN all day. And right after that I realize it's still only Saturday. People might cut me some slack for my "maybe a minor concussion" today, but that still leaves all of Sunday and Sunday night.

I'm stuck. I look at the piles. I'll have to do all of it. Not tonight, though. I can give myself a break on that, even if it means more for tomorrow. I reach over with both hands and mess up all of the little piles.

Then I get a phone call.

"Yuh?" I say.

"Do you have a big bandage around your head?" says Tim, instead of hello. "Did they give you a brain transplant? Do you look like Frankenstein?"

"No, no," I say. "They said my brain was already too damaged to operate on. Even before the game."

"I could've told 'em that," he says. "But how are you, like, really?"

"I'm OK," I say. "Except I don't want to do my homework."

"I must've been hit in the head, too," he says. "Because I don't want to either."

Then he tells me about the game. Even though I already know about it from Andy, it's still cool, because Tim has different details. It's amazing how different the view can be from second base and third. Plus, Tim hit a triple. Triples are pretty rare on our team, more rare than home runs, even.

I get a few more e-mails than normal over the next day or so, and a bunch of my teammates call, which is even more unusual.

"I wanted to knock that big gorilla out cold," says Jackson.

I know he means it, because I remember him bumping into Tebow when they were all standing around me at the game. It seems like a good sign that I can remember that. No brain transplant for me.

Even J.P. calls. He doesn't say much, but it's still J.P. Coach calls an hour later, and I feel kind of like a rock star myself. Or at least like the bassist or drummer or something.

We all have each other's numbers from the team contact list. Most of my teammates don't call, of course. A lot of them probably hear I'm OK secondhand.

One of the people who doesn't call is Katie. On Sunday night, I open the drawer on my computer desk and take out the team contact list. It seems funny that her name is right there: Bowe, Kathryn. I sort of wonder why it says

Kathryn and not Katie. Did she give Coach that name to use for the list, or was it her parents? Does she prefer Kathryn, and just no one calls her that, or is it just because this is like an official team document?

I think that's something I could ask her. But I can't call her. It's not like she was hit in the head. And even if I ask her in school, what would I say: "I was just staring at your name on the team contact list"?

I could just pick up the phone right now and call Andy, but calling Katie — Kathryn? — would be this big thing. It would be this Big Thing, and everyone would be talking about it.

I put the list back in the drawer and go back to my homework. Man, I think. I should've done some of this yesterday.

Chapter

19

I sort of know I'm dreaming, or I half know, anyway. Dreams can be so weird that way. I sort of know it's a dream, and I sort of already know what's going to happen, but I can't stop it, and I can't help freaking out about it.

I'm standing in the batter's box at Culbreath Field, our practice field. I'm looking out at the mound, and there's a pitcher going into his windup. He's big, but I can't see his face so I don't know if it's that kid Tebow or someone else. I don't recognize his uniform, either, but his arm is coming up, and now I've got bigger problems.

I go to pick up my front foot, just a little to start timing my swing, but *my foot won't budge*. I try harder to pick it up, and nothing happens. It's like it's glued there. I try to step back out of the box, but now my other foot won't move, either. I'm completely stuck!

The pitcher's arm is coming forward. His arm is big and powerful, and I just know he's going to launch the ball like a rocket. I'm jerking both legs now, trying to move my feet even an inch. Nothing happens. I'm stuck in place. It's like I'm waist-deep in mud.

As the huge figure on the mound delivers the pitch, I can finally see his face. It's blank. I don't mean his expression, I mean his face! There is nothing there: no mouth, no nose, no eyes. I want to scream out, but I can't. I want to move, but I can't do that, either. The ball is coming straight for me, straight for my head. Of course it is. I knew all along it would. All I can do is take it.

I wake up sweating and jittery. For a long time I just lie there, staring straight up at the ceiling. It's blank, too. Every once in a while, I move my feet under the covers.

Chapter

20

I'm waiting for the bus on Monday morning, looking down Main Street for something big and yellow. It's a little warmer today, even though it's still so-so-so early. Why does school have to start so early? Right on cue, the bus pulls up, and its door opens. Shut up and get in, it says.

My stop is kind of late on the route, so I almost always have to sit with someone. It isn't always someone I want to sit with, either. There are other guys from the team on the bus, but they're usually already two to a seat by then. Andy would save a seat for me, but he takes a different bus.

Today I sit with Zeb Chamberlain. Zeb is short for Zebediah. I didn't even think that was a real name before I met him. I mean, I knew there was Zachariah and I knew there was Jedediah, but Zebediah? What, did Zachariah and Jedediah have a kid?

Anyway, he's OK. He plays for another Tall Pines team, the Rockies. I'm glad I don't play for the Rockies. That name just seems geographically stupid around here. We were much better than the Rockies last year, too. I should know: We played them often enough.

We'll find out pretty soon who's better this year. We're playing them next. Sitting with Zeb isn't a big deal, though, not like if I was caught hanging out with someone from the Haven Yankees. The Rockies are from the same town, go to the same school, and ride the same buses. It would be impossible to avoid them, so we don't really try.

Still, you don't necessarily want to sit next to them the week of a game. Of course you're going to talk about baseball — what else would you talk about? — and you don't want to give anything away. I don't have a choice, though.

"Heard you got plunked," Zeb says, first thing.

"Yep," I say. The side of my head is still sore enough that I'm not wearing my Braves cap like I usually do on the bus.

"It hurt?" says Zeb.

"I got my bell rung," I say. "No biggie."

I'm trying not to think about it, and that's as much as he needs to know, anyway.

I catch up with Andy at his locker. We're in sixth grade now, but we still have the little mini lockers that are "sized appropriately" for elementary school. I think the best thing about junior high is going to be having lockers that don't look like they're from the Munchkin Land of Oz. Anyway, we go over our math homework super quick because it was kind of tricky.

He looks at the side of my head once or twice, but that's it. It's not like there's anything to see. But people keep doing that all day. About a dozen times I feel like saying, It's fine, all right?

Before lunch, a kid who's maybe in fourth grade walks up to me and just stands there. He clearly has something to say, so I go, "What?"

"I heard your brains were coming out of your ears," he says.

I can't tell if he's joking. Maybe he really believes it. I don't remember our science lessons being all that great in fourth grade.

"Who said that?" I ask, even though I have a pretty good idea.

"Bye," he says, and walks away.

Little punk.

Anyway, I figure all I have to do is get through this one day, then everybody will be over it. There will be something else to talk and gawk about tomorrow.

And that's what I do, just get through the school day. The second half goes better than the first. There's big news. Everyone is talking about how Benny Mills farted doing pull-ups in gym class.

It's kind of a funny story — funnier than getting hit in the head, anyway. It was that physical fitness test we have to take, so only three kids go at a time, and Ms. Cimino is right there counting. I mean, on sit-ups, the spotter counts, because some kids can really fly on that. I did forty-five in a minute, and that wasn't even the best. But on pull-ups, Cimino could be playing a video game and still count three of us. A lot of kids can't even do one. (I did three. It's not exactly a world record. But still, I did three.)

We hear the story from Dustin, who was there. "So Benny's really struggling, right?" he says. It's lunch, and he's got the whole table's full attention. "You know, he's cranking away on pull-up number one, maybe halfway there. His face is bright red and scrunched up."

Dustin stops and scrunches up his face to demonstrate.

"Dude, you look constipated," says Andy.

"I'm getting to that part!" says Dustin. "So anyways, the other kids've pretty much packed it in after cranking out as many pull-ups as they could. Not many. So everyone is just watching Benny and waiting for Cimino to click her stopwatch and put him out of his misery."

Dustin stops and looks around the table. He's building up the suspense, so we know that whatever he's got to say is going to be good.

"Yeah?" says Tim.

"OK," says Chester.

"And then: *Brrrriippp!*" says Dustin. "*BRRRRIIPPP!* He just lets one go! Lets. One. Go. I guess he was just so clenched up that he squeezed it out without even realizing. And what could he do? He's just hanging there, like, on display. It's not like he can pretend someone else did it."

"No way!" Andy and I say at the same time.

"Wow," says Tim, sitting back from the table like he's just witnessed some kind of tragedy.

"Yeah," says Dustin, nodding solemnly. "Yeah. So Cimino just clicks the watch, either because time really was up or because she was standing right in the waft zone, and that's it. Game over. Benny just drops down from the bar, as good as dead."

"And you saw this?" says Tim. "All of it?"

"Saw it?" says Dustin. "I *smelled* it!"

Dustin pops up, grabs his tray, and takes it over to the next table. He's like our Paul Revere, spreading the word far and wide. For the rest of the day, no one is talking about me getting beaned anymore. In the war movies, that's what they call covering fire. I should thank Benny, but I don't really know him. And everyone knows to steer clear of him today, anyway.

So things are going along fine. Then, at the end of the day, right before the buses, Tim says, "Bet you can't wait to get back to practice tomorrow."

I hadn't really thought about it until then. I'd been thinking about everyone staring at me, and getting through classes, and then swapping stories about Benny. I mean, I knew practice was tomorrow, but I hadn't really been thinking about what that meant. It means putting a helmet on my bruised-up head and stepping into the box.

And you might think I'd say, "Heck, yeah," or something like that, but I don't say anything. I just give Tim this blank look like he might as well be talking to a goldfish.

"Well," says Tim, once he gets tired of waiting, "see ya tomorrow."

"Yeah," I say. "See ya in the a.m."

But that's all I say. I have this weird feeling in my gut.

What is that? I think. It feels like . . . and then it comes to me: It feels like after that dream.

Chapter

21

I wake up nervous on Tuesday morning. It feels like game day, but it also feels different. I try not to think too much about it. Let's be honest: There are plenty of things to be nervous about on a day-to-day basis in sixth grade.

I get dressed and tell my brain to shut up. It gets revenge by dressing me stupidly. Even though it's not that cold, I put on a big blue sweater. I know I'm going to end up sitting next to the windows in math and baking, but I put it on anyway. I just wear a good T-shirt underneath, instead of one of the white ones with holes, so I can ditch the sweater if I need to. By the time I leave the house, I'm like an advertisement for the color blue: blue jeans, blue sweater, and my dark blue Braves cap, which fits again.

Tuesday is back to normal at school, with no one hit in the head or farting in the gym. It goes fast, and pretty soon I'm sitting next to Andy on the cool grass of Culbreath Field.

After a game, Coach always starts off with a postmortem. That means, like, an autopsy. It's a good name for it, too, because it can be as tough to stomach if we lose. Not that I've cut up a lot of corpses. And we didn't lose, either. But there are always things to go over — win, lose, or lose badly.

All three coaches talk during the postmortem, and pretty much none of the players do. Last year, I was always afraid they were going to single me out for some mistake, but there's not much they can say to me today.

"How's the coconut, Mogens?" Coach says right at the start.

"Fine," I say, and I knock on it twice with my knuckles.

That's pretty much it for me, but a few other kids take it on the chin. I guess there were some problems with players not backing up the cutoff throws.

"Throws going to third from right," says Coach. "Who's the cutoff?"

"Me, Coach," says Tim. "Second baseman."

And the way he says it, you know he didn't do it right on at least one play on Saturday.

"Could've fooled me," says Coach, sort of twisting the knife a little. Meanwhile, Tim's dad is looking at his son like he's bailing him out of jail.

"And who's backing up third?" Coach says, like he can't believe he even has to ask.

"Pitcher, Coach," says J.P.

"What's that, J.P.?" Coach says, even though there's no way he didn't hear.

"PITCHER, Coach," says J.P.

So J.P. shuts out the other team, and Coach is grilling him about not backing up third on the one time a runner got that far. It seems kind of crazy, right? But Coach has a point, and we all sort of know it. If the ball gets away at third, and there's no one there to back up the throw, the runner probably scores.

And more than that, a few extra bases here and there might not mean that much in a 7–0 game. But that's exactly how you lose a close game. It's how we lost to Haven last year. So everyone, even J.P., just takes their medicine.

And sure enough, we spend almost half of practice working on cutoff throws and backing up bases.

"Grab the tub," Coach yells at no one in particular. That's what he calls the big plastic trash can we use for throws home, instead of killing our catchers with one-hoppers and high-flyers and everything in between.

Everyone groans, but not me. I want to be in the field. I bust it out to left before Geoff can get there. I'm still the starter, as far as I know. You don't lose your spot due to injury. That's like universal. Otherwise people would play it safe all the time, just trying not to get hurt.

Geoff knows the deal and doesn't make it a foot race. The coaches are going to shift us all over the field anyway, so we'll know what to do wherever we play.

"Don't make me look bad," Andy says as he breaks off for third base. He's smiling, but he means it. If the ball is hit down the line and the throw is going home, he's my cutoff man.

"Incoming!" I say, because when I miss, I usually overthrow, like artillery. I'm smiling, too, but what I mean is, I'll do my best.

And then we're out there: the starting lineup from Saturday. Some of us are hoping not to repeat our mistakes, and some of us are just glad to be out in the field again. Coach is tossing the balls up and hitting them. J.P. is just out there to field.

The first fly ball goes to Manny in center. The crack of the bat hits me like a punch to the stomach. That's when I realize how much I don't want to bat today.

I watch Manny camp out under the lazy fly ball, squaring himself to throw. It looks so harmless in the air like that, but I don't want to see it at the plate. Manny makes the catch, and Tim pounds his fist into his glove, waiting to get the throw. It's on-line, and he catches it cleanly, spins, and throws a one-hopper over the mound and into the plastic trash can.

"There ya go, Liu!" yells Coach. "That so hard?"

This is a problem: a big, fat problem. But the next ball is hit to me, and I don't think about anything else.

I shade over toward the line. The ball is basically coming right to me, but I take a step back. You want to be behind the ball and coming forward in order to make a strong throw. You definitely don't want to be backpedaling.

I line it up so that I'm stepping forward as I make the catch. I get the ball out of my glove quick and throw it on a line to Andy.

Sure enough, I overthrow him. Ugh. He bails me out by jumping for it and making a snow-cone catch with the very top of his glove. He comes down with it just as Coach finishes turning the can toward third. Andy throws it in there on the fly.

"You benchwarmers watching this?" Coach yells, meaning the starters are doing it right.

Andy turns and points to me, as if my throw had been perfect. I know it wasn't, but I point back, glad my best friend is also our best third baseman.

The next ball goes to right.

"Play is to third!" Coach yells.

J.P. is off the mound and backing up the throw in a heartbeat.

I move over to take a turn in center field and then to right and then take a seat on the bench. Geoff is one behind me the whole time: in left when I'm in center, in center when I'm in right. By the time he makes it to right, the drill is over.

"BP!" yells Coach. "Let's see if you knuckleheads can still hit."

The nerves come back like a wave breaking over top of me. My heart feels too big for my chest, and my lungs feel too small. It's like there's too much blood getting to my head and not enough oxygen. For the first time in my life, I'm hoping practice ends before I get my turn at bat.

BP starts like it always does: Everyone out in the field. I grab the glove that I just put down a few minutes ago and head out to join the crowd in left. It's the place to be because it's where most of the balls are hit. This I can do.

Coach looks around and calls you in for your turn. No one's ever sure how he comes up with the order. It seems kind of random, and I guess maybe that's the point. If all the best hitters went first, then the last kids to go would know they sucked, instead of just suspecting it.

Anyway, Jackson is first up. He's a right-handed pull hitter, and he usually puts on a show, so I pound my fist into my glove and get ready. Coach Liu is pitching to give Wainwright a break after hitting all those balls.

Coach Liu's pitches are a little flatter and straighter than Coach's lollipops.

Harder, too. It just pops into my brain. I want to make a catch right now, to chase down a fly ball slicing toward the line. I just want to do something to not think so much, but Jackson is waiting on the pitches like he should. He's driving them more toward center. His third shot clears the fence, and everyone hoots and whoops.

I watch Jackson: how relaxed he looks, how easy his swing is. He cranks a few more, and Coach has seen enough. He calls in one of the new kids. Good luck following that. He doesn't come close, but he gives the infield a workout, which is probably what Coach is looking for.

J.P. goes next, and his power seems to be down a little. He's working on making contact. Wayne is up next. He's Malfoy's friend and Andy's competition at third, so: double evil. Then it's Katie: double good. She hits one right to me, and I pretend she meant to. I smile for the first time all day, and then I hear my name.

The smile is gone and the nerves are back. I put my head down and jog in. Mind over matter, that's what Dad would say: I don't mind and you don't matter. My body will do what I tell it to. I hope.

The helmet slips on. It's not the one I usually wear, because that's the one I got hit in. And I guess it did its job, but I don't even want to look at it right now. The new one fits OK, and I barely feel it as it slides over the bruise.

I put on my batting glove and pick up the bat I like. Katie takes her last swing, and I'm up. Everything feels fast and out of control. It's not until the first pitch is coming in that I realize I didn't go through my routine.

The pitch is outside. Thank God. I reach out and bounce it to one of the extra infielders on the right side. Lame. Then the next pitch comes in on me. It's maybe an inch or two inside, but it's the kind of pitch that would be called a strike nine times out of ten. I just need to keep my arms in, but I don't keep anything in.

The pitch has a little tailing action, and in my head it seems like it's coming straight for me. I jump back out of the way, and the thing misses me by two feet.

"What was that?" Liu shouts from the mound.

"Nothing," I say. "Got fooled."

Yeah, fooled by a flat BP fastball. That's believable.

Liu gives me a weird look, winds up, and tosses another.

This one is right down the middle, and I handle it a little better.

The next one is outside, and I hit a solid liner. It gets caught by one of the extra fielders, but it probably would've been a base hit in a normal game. I start to feel a little better. I even take my little mini swings before the next pitch. And then Liu comes inside. Not much, but it's enough.

I bail out completely, sticking my bat out toward the plate as I throw my shoulders back out and away from it. The ball just doinks off the end.

I look up, and I realize something: Coach Liu knows. He saw me jump off the plate on a pitch just inside. Then he went middle, then away, and watched me put two decent swings on the ball. Then he came back in.

Just to make sure, he comes in again. I don't even offer at it. I take a good, hittable pitch in batting practice. Right now, I'd give anything for that weak chopper I hit on the first pitch, the one I thought was so lame. I can't believe this. I'm bailing out on everything inside.

"What is going on, Mogens?" yells Coach Wainwright from the side of the cage.

"Nothing, Coach," I say.

"Yeah," he says. "That pretty well sums it up."

He calls Manny in to bat next.

I slink back out into the field. If Coach hasn't figured it out already, Liu will let him know what's up afterward.

Manny doesn't make eye contact. He looks down as we pass each other. He's embarrassed for me. I trade my batting glove for my real one. And the worst part: I'm glad it's over. I should be dying for another swing, but I'm not. I head out to left, and no one says anything to me as I go.

I hear someone laughing off in the distance. I don't need to look up to know that it's Malfoy.

I try to settle myself down in the field. A few batters later, Chester hits one in the air. It's practically a home run for him, but really, it's a blooper to shallow left. It's dropping fast, right in front of me. I should stay back and play this one on the hop. That's the smart thing to do, but I'm still burning with embarrassment. This seems like just what I need.

I break into a flat-out sprint. Maybe I can make this catch. Maybe the coaches can talk about that after practice, about my glove. Maybe I can make Malfoy swallow some of that laughter. There's no way he'd make this catch.

I'm running as fast as I can, starting to lean forward and get low as I go. My hat flies backward off my head. The ball is sinking fast. I'm almost there. Everything is converging: the ball, the grass, my glove. . . .

I dive for it.

I miss.

Chapter 23

"Man, you were awesome out there yesterday," Andy says.

We're sitting at our normal table in the cafeteria, and someone was going to have to say something about it sooner or later.

"Yeah," I say. "Thanks. I hope you guys understand I'm not trying to show you up or anything."

"No, no, no," says Tim. "A star has gotta shine, right?"

"Yeah," I say. "Exactly."

"Heck of a catch out there, too," says Chester, who made it all the way to third after my diving miss. If I'd stayed back, like a non-brain-damaged player, it would've been a single.

They're going easy on me. After six years of mostly good practices, I guess maybe I get a pass for one really bad one. But they don't know what I know, what Coach Liu knows. I change the subject.

"I was watching this show on cable last night, about rodents," I say. That's about as far away from the subject as it can get. It might be a little too far away. As soon as I say it, I'm afraid they're just going to let it drop and go back to talking about practice. But Andy bails me out.

"Oh, yeah," he says. "On Discovery?"

I know he's just guessing, acting like he saw it, but no one else does. It's a pretty solid guess. It would be either that or Animal Planet.

"Yeah," I say.

"Like *Most Extreme: Rodents*, right?" he says, doubling down. "Yeah, that was cool."

"Extreme rodents?" says Tim, and now the ball is rolling. "That's ridiculous!"

"Yeah, yeah," says Dustin, who has started sitting with us most days. "Oh, no, a gerbil!"

"No, but a rat can squeeze through a hole the size of a quarter," I say. "And chew through concrete."

"No way!" says Andy, already forgetting that he was supposed to have watched the show.

"Yuh-huh," I say. "And they're the deadliest animal in history."

"What?" says Dustin. "You have lost it. Seriously."

"Nope, it's true. Because they spread disease. Like the Great Plague wiped out millions of people, and that was because of rats."

"Nuh-uh," says Tim. "Fleas."

"Yeah, but the fleas were on the rats," I say. "That's how the disease spread so far."

"Yeah, but it was still the fleas that carried it," says Tim. "So why aren't fleas the World's Deadliest Animal in History?"

And then we get into a long, kind of dumb discussion about whether insects are animals or just, you know, insects. That's fine with me. I'd rather talk about that than my meltdown at practice.

It's not until the end of lunch that we get back to baseball, and then it's to talk about the next game. The five of us are clearing away our trays and heading out. We're talking about the Rockies, and they're, you know, "all around us," so we can't be giving away any trade secrets. Still, Dustin wants to know what we think about our chances, so we tell him.

"Yeah, I think we got 'em," says Andy.

"Yeah, mos' def," says Tim.

We haven't played them yet, but we see those guys around all the time. I have to wait to give my take until their starting catcher walks past. Dustin nods to him in that yeah-I-have-to-wear-all-that-gear-too way. And I know he's the Rockies' starter this year because he's in my gym class. He nods back at Dustin and then at me.

Once he's gone, I start talking. "Yeah, I like our chances," I say. "But they've got some decent players."

Then I think of something else: "And we won't have J.P. on the mound — at least not until Malfoy gets knocked out in the third!"

The others laugh, except for Tim. I can see his eyes get wide. Oh, man, I think, and I turn around. Sure enough, there's Malfoy, right behind us.

Oh, man . . .

I turn back quick, and Tim is looking right at me. I mouth the words: *Did he hear?*

Tim just shrugs. I risk another quick look over my shoulder, but Malfoy's gone. He took the turnoff toward the library.

"Whoops!" I say, and Tim chuckles.

"What?" says Andy.

"Malfoy was right behind us!" says Tim.

The rest of them look back, but that only confirms that he's not there anymore.

"Really?" says Dustin.

"Yep," I say.

"Ooooooh!" they say. Chester starts it, and they all join in.

"He's gonna be steamed," says Dustin. "That's like" — and he pauses to count — "three disses in one."

It's true. Strike one: I called him Malfoy, which he hates. Strike two: I basically said straight out that J.P. is vastly superior to him, which he isn't willing to admit.

And strike three: I said he'd get roughed up and knocked out of the game. Yeah, that's bad.

"Maybe he didn't even hear," I say.

And maybe he didn't. I mean, it's possible. Maybe he wasn't even paying attention. Maybe he was thinking about, I don't know, potions class or something.

I'm hoping more than thinking, though. I've got enough trouble without that: He's our number two pitcher and Coach Meacham's number one son and a giant jerk-butt, anyway. Plus, well, I haven't really mentioned this yet, but we've kind of got a history, Malfoy and I. I'm just starting to think about that when Dustin sums things up.

"He's going to be steamed," Dustin repeats, like the case is settled. He thinks he knows Malfoy best because he catches him. I know he doesn't. Like I said, we've got that history. That's how I know that steamed wouldn't even begin to cover it.

Chapter 24

We head back to our lockers. Chester and Tim peel off, leaving Dustin, Andy, and me.

"Can't believe I did that," I say.

"Did what?" says Dustin. He's honestly stumped for a second, even though it was just a few minutes ago. "Oh, the thing with Malfoy? Don't sweat it."

"You're the one who said he was going to be so mad," I remind him.

"Yeah, but who are we talking about here?" says Dustin. "He's always mad."

"Good point," I say. I want to say more, but we've reached Dustin's locker.

Now it's just Andy and me. He's the one guy I don't have to explain this to.

"Not good," he says.

"Nope," I say.

"Déjà vu," he says.

"Yep," I say.

And then he ducks his head into his locker, and I'm alone in the hallway.

I'm thinking about what happened with Malfoy. I don't mean five minutes ago, I mean five years. I'll just say it: Malfoy and I used to be best friends. That's the history. This was like kindergarten and first grade. I guess, if you want to look at it that way, he was my first best friend. "Meach," that's what I called him back then.

Malfoy and I — Meach, whatever — it's not like we had a big argument or anything. I mean, he was always a little out there. I remember once, in kindergarten, he cut all the limbs off one of the playtime dolls with those green-handled safety scissors. He cut it up and left it there for the girls to find. He did that just the one time, but there were other things.

It wasn't really that stuff, though. I just met Andy in second grade, and we got along better. Maybe we had more in common or something, I don't know. It was second grade. But those two didn't get along at all, and so there I was: monkey in the middle. And I made my choice.

Chapter
25

When I get home it's like, good sweet lord, all I want to do is get to my room, you know? After a long day of changing the topic and maybe being overheard and maybe not, I just want to go upstairs, close the door, and kill something in a video game. But as soon as I drop my backpack onto the chair in the living room, there's Dad. He's working from home today, which he does sometimes. I guess I'd forgotten.

"Hey," I say.

"Hey," he says, but there's a little smile creeping onto his face, and both of his hands are behind his back, so I know something is going on.

"What?" I say.

"What?" he says, and I start searching my brain.

What does he have behind his back? If he'd seen me at

practice yesterday, or if I'd had the guts to tell him about it, it would be a gun to put me out of my misery. But he didn't see me, and that wouldn't explain the smile. Mercy killing or not, he'd at least feel guilty about it.

And then I remember: It's a new baseball season. I don't mean Little League; I mean Major League Baseball. It's a new season, and I know what he's got back there. As soon as Dad sees it click in my mind, he brings them out. His smile is ear to ear now, and he's holding half a dozen packs of brand-new baseball cards.

Right then, my brain literally splits in half. Seriously, it's like half of it squeezes out one ear and heads toward the stairs. That half is still bummed out and wants to be left alone. But the other half squeezes out the other ear and heads over to the couch. That half wants to see the cards.

I just stand there for a second with no brain left in my head. The smile on my dad's face twitches a little. Before it can collapse altogether, the bummed-out half of my brain gives in and heads for the couch, too.

"Cool," I say, forcing a smile.

Before long we're sitting on the couch, and we have the coffee table cleared off to make room. It doesn't require a single word between us. We've been doing this every year for most of my life. Dad gets me a big handful of the new cards each season.

Then we spread them out and look for good play-ers and, especially, rookie cards. It's like some weird combination of Christmas morning, opening day, and an Easter egg hunt.

The tabletop is clear, and the cards are in a little pile between Dad and me.

"Ready?" he says.

"Ready," I say.

"Ready?" he says again, louder.

"Ready!"

By now, the bummed-out half of my brain has given in, and it's sitting there with a big doofy smile on its face, too. With no objections, I tear open the first pack. At the last second, I remember to wipe my hands on my jeans. It can mean the difference between near mint condition and mint. Then I start spreading the first pack of cards out face up.

"Oooh!" Dad says as I slap down a good one.

"All-Star!" I say a few cards later.

A few clunkers later, Dad says, "Rookie card!"

"Guy's a scrub," I say.

"Might surprise you," says Dad.

"Doubt it."

But a few cards into the second pack, a good one comes up. It's another rookie, for the Cubs, but this guy is supposed to be the real deal.

Dad makes that Homer Simpson drooling noise and pretends to reach for it. My mouth is occupied trying to break down the fossilized bubble gum that came in one of the packs. I smack the back of his hand instead.

"But I wants it," he says. He's gone from Homer Simpson to imitating Gollum from the *Lord of the Rings* movies. "I *wants* it!"

"Get your own!" I say.

"I've got my own," he says, and I know what's coming next. "In fact, when I was just about your age now, I got my Ripken."

Dad's Cal Ripken, Jr., rookie card . . . He brings it up every year. Ripken is in the Hall of Fame now, and the card is in the mini safe in the basement, along with the title to the house and some old jewelry from my mom's mom.

That's the pot of gold, the Holy Grail, the, well, you get the idea. We're looking for the next one of those. I want a card to put in the safe. Usually, when he mentions his Ripken, it's like rocket fuel for me to go through the rest of the cards.

But now I slow down, stop. I'm thinking about a TV show I saw on Ripken. He's baseball's all-time iron man. He played in 2,632 straight games, all for the Orioles. That's one of those numbers that a lot of baseball fans just know, like 4,256, Pete Rose's record for hits.

"Two thousand six hundred and thirty-two," I say.

"Yeah," says dad. "With three thousand one hundred and eighty-four hits and four hundred and thirty-one homers."

Most fans don't know those stats, except maybe Orioles fans.

"Unbelievable," I say.

"Believe it," says Dad. "I saw a few of them."

But that's not what I mean. I mean, all those games . . . How many times was he hurt or injured? How many times did he get hit by a pitch, not just off the thigh or butt, but somewhere it hurt? And he never missed a beat.

Right then, I know two things. One: If Cal Ripken got hit in the head by a pitch, he would pick himself up and head down to first base. There wouldn't be a cloud of people hovering over him and tears in his eyes and a pinch-runner who got thrown out at home. And he definitely wouldn't bail out on inside pitches three days later. Just the thought of it is ridiculous. I mean, please: Inside pitches would bail out on him!

And so that's the other thing I know. Two: I'm not like Cal Ripken. I'm not a baseball player like him. Now I'm not smiling at all. The same card has been pinched between my fingers for too long, getting oil on the cardboard. The gum has run out of flavor in my mouth. It just tastes like spit so I swallow it.

"What's up, champ?" Dad says, finally noticing.

"Don't call me that," I say.

I slap the card down on the table. It's nobody special. Figures.

Chapter 26

"What is your major malfunction?" Andy says. It's a line from a movie, but you get the idea. He's asking what's wrong with me.

"What do you mean?" I say, even though I mean, duh.

We're loosening up and stretching before practice on Thursday. With Andy and me, that also means loosening up and stretching our jaws. His mom just dropped us off like a minute ago.

"What do you mean, 'What do you mean?'" he says. "You know what I mean!"

"Yeah," I say, shrugging and throwing a ball into my mitt. "Maybe."

"Maybe, my bouncing baboon butt," he says. Improving on the words *my butt* is a big thing with the guys in our grade this year. "You've been moping around all week."

136

"I haven't been moping!" I say.

But he's right. Andy has had to put up with it the whole time, so he doesn't let it slide. He just lists half a dozen things I've done, haven't done, said, or haven't said. Andy's a smart guy. I don't know if I mentioned that yet, but he is. And he has a good memory.

"And Chester took *all* your Tater Tots and you didn't even say anything! And Chester is like three feet tall! And then, right after that —"

"All right, all right," I say, cutting him off. I can't stomach any more of the evidence. "I'm not moping," I say again. "I'm just, you know, open to mopin'."

Andy gives me a weird look, like he didn't hear me right. Then he laughs.

"Open to mopin'," he says. "That's pretty good. Where did you hear that?"

"Nah, just made it up," I say, and it's true. Right on the spot. The mind can come up with some clever stuff when it's trying to avoid the truth.

"Well, that's pretty good," Andy says. A thoughtful look comes over his face and he adds, "Considering how stupid you are."

Now I laugh, because I really thought he was going to say something nice there.

"Get your glove on," I say, holding up the ball like I'm playing fetch with Nax.

"Yeah, all right," he says. "Open to mopin' . . ."

And then he says it: "I may even allow you to serve as a rifleman in my beloved corps."

It's another line from the same movie. I'm not saying which movie because it's not exactly rated G. But Andy bought it for two bucks at the Winter Fair at our church, so it's not like it's that bad. It's just a war movie.

But anyway, the thing is, if you begin with that first line, you have to end with that second one. That makes it official. Unless you still have a "major malfunction," so what Andy is saying is that I don't. And you know what? I sort of do feel better about things now. War movies kind of put things in perspective.

Other kids are arriving. Chester comes over to see if we want to toss the ball around three ways.

"Nah," says Andy. "We're just gonna long toss. My arm is all, like, tight."

Chester looks over at me, hoping for a second opinion.

"Hit the road," I say.

Chester waves his glove at us like we're both useless and starts walking away.

"Tot thief," I add.

He waves his glove at us again, this time behind his back, and walks on.

Andy and I just toss the ball back and forth without another word. The only sounds are the pop of the baseball landing in our gloves, the cars whooshing by out on

Maplewood, and the scattered chatter around us. Then Coach arrives and practice begins.

I don't feel the same nerves I did on Tuesday, or at least I don't feel them quite so much. I'm starting to think I'm going to be OK.

Famous last words.

Chapter 27

We start out with the star drill. It's the exact same drill we used to call hot potato a few years ago. It's a little confusing. Like if someone misses practice and asks what we did, you might say, "We started off with the star drill," and they'd say, "You mean hot potato?" and you'd say, "Yeah." It's just that we're older now. You've got to have some self-respect.

Anyway, the drill is pretty simple. You break up into groups of five and get in a circle. Then you toss the ball to the person two to your left. They call it the star drill because the ball travels in a star shape by the time it gets back to the first guy.

The first thing is, you want five good guys. Andy and I are already standing next to each other, so there's two. But it's a scramble after that, because the good partners get snapped up. So it's like: Here's Chester again.

He latched on with Tim and Dustin, so that's the three we need. I try to make eye contact with one of them, but there are already kids heading for them. Andy takes a few quick steps, but he's not going to get there in time. If they add even one more kid, they'll have four, and the two of us will have to keep fishing.

So I throw my glove. It hits Tim in the back of the legs.

"Hey!" he says, spinning around.

"Nice arm," says Andy.

The first kid is talking to Dustin, but Tim turns to him and says, "Nah, we're set."

Dustin looks up, like: We are? And Tim just points his glove at Andy and me, hustling up. Chester smirks. "Oh, noooww you two want some of my sweet, sweet glovin'," he says.

So we luck out and get a good group. We form a circle and start out pretty close in.

"Toss it!" yells Coach.

We flip the ball to each other fast, like we're getting the ball out of our gloves to turn a double play. We've got Andy, Tim, and Chester: all top-of-the-line infielders. And Dustin and I have both spent time there, too, and we've been doing this drill since, you know, hot potato. So we're flying.

Toss; catch, transfer, toss; catch, transfer, toss; catch, transfer, toss; catch, transfer, toss; and we're done, and we start again, even faster.

Coach Liu wanders by. It looks like he's going to say something, but he doesn't, probably because of Tim being here. He notices, though. You can see he's impressed. When he walks away, we exchange smiles as we follow the ball around the circle.

"Back it up!" Coach yells out.

We make the last toss, back to the guy who made the first throw. Dustin holds the ball, and we make the circle wider.

"Grounders!" yells Coach.

I groan. Great: I've got three awesome infielders and the starting catcher. These guys eat bad hops for lunch. Me? I'm an outfielder, all right? Most balls come to me airmail, and the ones on the ground are usually all out of tricks by the time I can get a glove on them.

So you'd think I'd be concentrating, right? Well, I am — until I see Katie in the next group over. What? She's a great infielder. Seriously. And OK, there's something about how her ponytail flies around, and her —

"Heads up!"

But with grounders that really means heads down. My eyes go the wrong way, but my body has done this drill before. I fall down to my knees to smother the ball. It bounces up into my chest.

"Ooooof!" I say as it rolls away. I scramble after it, and the other guys are laughing.

"Nice play," says Tim. "Maybe you should just tape the glove to your chest."

"They could call you Chester, too," says Chester.

Yeah, ha-ha-ha. I drill the ball into the ground in front of Tim. I throw it extra hard, but he vacuums it up like it's nothing.

I swivel my head in every direction: Did Coach see? Katie? When the next ball comes, I'm ready. It was another dumb mistake, though, like diving for that ball on Tuesday, like bailing out at the plate. My cold streak is becoming an ice age.

And I still have to bat.

I'm waiting for it all practice, but I'm thinking we'll just do batting practice. Since Tuesday, I've been thinking what I could do differently, how I could get myself to stay in on those inside pitches. How I could convince myself or trick myself or just anything.

We motor right through the middle of practice, and long after the star drill ends, we're still in the field. I know from the postmortem there were some errors against Haven, so Coach is making a point of "the fundamentals" today.

Still no BP, and I know what that means.

Katie, Tim, and Jackson turn a sweet double play. Coach finally seems satisfied.

"Live batting," he calls. "Let's get ready for those Rockies."

Live batting . . . Not everyone will bat. Maybe I can slip by. Maybe I can even still start. It was really just one bad practice.

I can't help myself. I look over at Coach. He gives me just the tiniest nod of his head, and my heart lands somewhere down by my cleats. I'll be batting, all right. Coach has been doing this too long to miss something so obvious. He needs to know what I've got for Saturday. He needs to know if he needs a new left fielder.

"Meacham!" Coach shouts. "Take the mound."

Malfoy sprints in from right, a wicked smile on his face and his glove up for the ball.

Chapter

28

"Cuddy, Jiménez, Mogens," says Coach. "We'll start off with you three. Grab a bat."

So right away, I'm in the hole, up third, and Geoff just jogs out to left without anyone needing to say anything. It doesn't settle who's going to get the start on Saturday, but I guess maybe that's the point.

Anyway, this is Three Bears batting. Coach does this a lot. Dustin is big, the papa bear, a power hitter. Chester is little, the baby bear. And I guess that makes me just right. We'll find out. I can already feel the churning in my stomach.

There are just too many things to try not to think about: getting hit on Saturday, lying there with tears in my eyes, going to the hospital. Getting humiliated at BP on Tuesday. The last one sneaks up on me: The last time

I faced Malfoy, he knocked me down. I can literally feel my pulse shift gears when I remember that, him pumping his fist and glaring in at me.

I try to talk to Chester, just to distract myself, but he's not having it. He's on deck and focused. Like I should be. I wander back to the pile of batting helmets and poke through it. I'm hoping there's one that covers my whole body.

Dustin steps to the plate, and I get a spot off to the side to try to time up Malfoy's pitches.

It's another nice evening, pretty warm, just a little wind. Malfoy is throwing easy, getting nice velocity. Dustin takes a few pitches, and it's one ball, one strike. Malfoy paints the outside corner to pull ahead in the count.

The outside corner, I think. Maybe he'll stay away. But that's just how you pitch to Dustin. He's a dead pull hitter and can turn on inside pitches like you wouldn't believe. Everyone knows to pitch him outside, and it occurs to me right then that I must be getting the opposite reputation.

Does everyone already know to pitch me inside? Half this team pitches or wants to, and it's the kind of thing we keep track of. It's weird; you think that what's going on with your swing is your business. Meanwhile, you've got a dozen kids watching you every time you pick up a bat.

Dustin is protecting the plate on the 1–2 pitch and swings at some junk. He chops it weakly to Katie, who guns him down by five steps.

Chester steps in and scrunches himself up. Malfoy looks in at that mini strike zone, but his expression doesn't change at all. Like I said, he's throwing easy today.

It's a long at-bat. My heart is racing the whole time. It doesn't seem possible that it could beat any faster and still be inside my chest. My hands are sweating so bad that I take off my batting glove, just so it doesn't turn into a water balloon.

I stuff the wrist end inside the waist of my practice pants and take a few light swings bare-handed. It feels wrong.

The count has been full for two pitches now. Malfoy is hitting the zone by taking a little off his fastball, daring Chester to make contact, but all Chester has managed to do so far is foul it off.

But Chester is getting comfortable now. He's figured out what Malfoy's doing, and there's a little smile on his face. He's going to wait on this next one. It's a mistake. Malfoy winds up big and launches one, blazing fast.

It's probably not a strike, but Chester is surprised by the velocity and doesn't do the math. He's way too late with a just-in-case hack and strikes out swinging.

Now I'm up. I'm fried. I feel like I do after a tough out, head down and beaten up, even though I haven't taken a single swing yet. I should have a white flag tied to the end of my bat.

Dustin has his catcher's gear on now and heads to the plate with me: me to hit (or not) and him to catch.

"Dude," he says. "Your glove."

I don't know what he means for a second. It's like I can barely hear him over the sound of the blood hammering in my head. Then I remember and look down. The fingers of my red and white batting glove are poking out of my pants, waving at me as I walk.

I barely have time to put it on before Malfoy goes into his windup. I don't even have time for one mini swing. He's coming right at me.

The first pitch is on the inside half. It's not way inside, but it still locks me up. I pick up the angle, the little cut inward, and I flinch. It's not much, but it's enough to ruin my balance. As a batter, you want to be like a cocked gun up there. That little flinch, it takes that away. And because the pitch still had plenty of the plate, it's an easy strike.

The second pitch is a rocket, and it's even farther inside. Malfoy has figured out the inside thing, just like Coach Liu. He was in right field for that and had a great view. And he knows me. He has for years. The only thing that keeps me from jumping back out of the box is the burning memory of how sick I felt after doing just that on

Tuesday. But all I can do is stand there. I am officially locked up.

Coach calls it a ball, and Dustin says, "Good eye," to me under his breath.

Good eye, my butt: My eyes were closed. It's 1–1.

I shake my head and shoulders, just to reset, and look out at the mound. Malfoy is working fast, already in his windup.

This one is way inside. I close my eyes again. I can feel the sweat inside my batting glove as I hear the ball pop into Dustin's mitt.

"Come on," yells someone in the field. And it's true: I'm not up there to test Malfoy's control. That was Chester's job. I'm up there to make contact, maybe hit a line drive. I used to be good at that. But here I am, a total statue, ahead in the count 2–1.

It doesn't make any sense. He could've struck me out by now. I look out to the mound a little earlier this time. I catch Malfoy's eyes. I see what's in them, and then I know. He's not trying to get me out. He's trying to punish me.

He goes into his windup, and I hold my breath because I know what's coming. I won't do it, though. Not again, and not now. I won't end another at-bat in the dirt.

The pitch comes in. It's a nasty snake of a fastball, hissing as it twists in toward me. The last thing that flashes through my mind is a single phrase, said just a little too loudly in the hallway after lunch.

I don't close my eyes this time. Why bother. I tilt my head back and look up at the gray sky as the ball drills me in the ribs.

That's it. I'm done. I'm never doing this again.

And then I drop to my knees. I've been taken apart, piece by piece.

Chapter 29

Afterward, everyone is like, "You should fight him! You should fight him!"

I think even he's expecting it, because he's hanging with Wayne and his one other friend on the team. We're all sitting on, hanging off, or standing around the bleachers, waiting for our marching orders for the game.

I'm standing with my usual group, off to one side. My ribs hurt, but I can tell they're not broken. I can tell because I can breathe without stabbing myself in the sides.

"Just go over there and punch him out!" Jackson is saying. "We got your back."

I look over at him and he means it. Even Chester is making fists with both hands, his glove on the ground in front of him. And the thing is, it's tempting. It really is. I'm hurting right now, and I don't mean my ribs. I mean

I'm embarrassed and beat down, and pounding on Malfoy doesn't sound so bad right now. But I'm not going to do it.

"Nah," I say, but they're waiting for more.

"Sometimes you squash the bug," I add. It's a saying we have and almost, like, a philosophy. The coaches are always telling us to "squash the bug" when we bat. It means to grind your weight down into the ground on that back foot as you swing, like there's a bug under it. So sometimes you squash the bug, and sometimes the bug squashes you. That's the rest of it. The bug can be the ball, the pitcher, the weather, your swing, whatever. It's a baseball explanation that can excuse a lot. Today, the bug won.

"OK," Chester says, still processing it. "After practice then?"

"Yeah!" says Tim. "After practice!"

"Yeah, yeah!" says Jackson.

And all of a sudden, it's like I agreed to it. The coaches are still walking slowly across the field from where they're huddled up, making their final decisions. In a few seconds, before they can get here, my friends will start telling other kids there's going to be a fight. Then there will be no going back.

That's how fights happen: just sheer momentum. It just snowballs all around you until it's like you've got no choice. But it's not what I want, and it's not going to make one bit of difference.

I look over at Andy, and I guess he was waiting for that, for confirmation one way or the other.

"No, no, no," he says. "He's not gonna fight after practice. Give him a break, he just got drilled in the ribs."

Everyone turns and looks at my ribs.

"Don't do it, man," Andy says, as if he's talking me out of it.

"All right," I say, fake-punching my fist into my glove.

Jackson makes the final decision. "Yeah," he says, disappointed. "Now is not the time."

And then the coaches arrive, turning the corner of the chain-link fence that separates the bleachers from the field. The first thing Coach Wainwright does is call out my name.

"Yeah," I say, but what I'm thinking is: What now?

The second thing he does is call Malfoy's.

"Yes, Coach," he says.

Coach makes a V with his first two fingers and points to both of us, on either side of the bleachers. It's like that gesture you make before you point at your own two eyes and then back out, meaning: I'm watching you.

"I don't know what it is with you two, but you better get it sorted," he says.

"What it is with *me*?" I want to say. I just got drilled in the ribs for no reason. And last time he knocked me down. That's what it is with me. But I don't say any of that. I just look at Coach when he looks at me.

153

He looks over at Malfoy, and that look lasts a little longer. Then he looks back at Coach Meacham, who doesn't say anything. Even *he* can't claim I was crowding the plate this time.

There's no official lineup, like last time, no calling out one through nine. Coach just makes a few replacements. I'm the first.

"How're the ribs, Mogens?" he starts.

"Fine," I say.

He squints at me and then looks at my side, as if injuries came with labels.

"How about the coconut?"

"Fine," I say.

I can feel a tear starting to form in the corner of my right eye. Not because of my ribs or my "coconut," but because I know what's coming next. I want to reach up and wipe it away, but everyone is looking at me and that would just call more attention to it. I just have to hope Coach gets this over with before the darn thing rolls down my cheek.

He sees it and does what he has to.

"Yeah, well, it's been a pretty rough stretch for you," he says quickly, rattling it off. "Better catch a breather. Kass . . ."

"Yeah, Coach," Geoff says from the middle of the bleachers.

"You got the start in left."

Everyone is looking at him now, and I reach up and wipe my glove across my face.

On the way home, I ask Dad whether we can go to McDonald's.

A lot of times he would just say no to that. Or not a lot of times because, truth is, I almost never ask anymore. Not like when I was younger and asked all the time. On the few times I've asked since majors, it's been about fifty-fifty.

Tonight, he takes one look over at me and says, "Sure, sport."

He doesn't ask why I want to go or why I'm being such a mopey lump or any of that. Open to mopin' . . . no kidding. He just makes the next right.

Once we get there, I order the fattiest fat food I can find. You know they have those "healthy" options, and I usually go for at least one of those. Like I'll get the apple wedges instead of fries and not even use the dipping sauce, or just a little, maybe.

Not tonight: I get the Big Mac meal and supersize it. I look up at my dad, because I sort of expect him to veto it, but he doesn't.

"What the heck," he says when it's his turn to order. "Number one, supersize."

He never does that. And I smile, just a little, as they start to fill up our trays. I carry my tray to a table by the window because we're eating here. "Destroying the evidence," Dad calls it, meaning Mom doesn't have to know.

We start to eat. We have the same thing, and I'm half his size, but I finish first. I pig out, like I've seen other kids do here for years, kids who aren't athletes. I look at my reflection in the window, two fries hanging out of my half-open mouth. What do I care?

Chapter

30

I stay up in my room and watch *Major League*. I don't know what's going on downstairs. I don't know if Dad is telling Mom we went to McDonald's and pigged out. She can probably smell it, anyway. The Big Mac is sitting in my stomach like a bowling ball.

Anyway, it's a funny movie, but I've seen it so many times that I don't really laugh at the jokes anymore. It's more like, I don't know, comforting? It's like I know all of the words, and I know when the boring parts are coming, with the broken-down old catcher trying to date the frizzy-haired lady. I can just follow along or read or go online or whatever. And it is funny, even if you don't laugh anymore, like when the catcher is reading the comic book of *Moby-Dick*. Plus, it's the TV version, so all the bad language is dubbed over in funny ways.

So I'm sort of watching it and sort of not, and suddenly it's that scene with Cerrano. You know, where he's hitting bombs out of the park, and the manager says: "This guy hits a ton. How come nobody else picked up on him?"

Then the other guy goes: "That's enough fastballs; throw him some breaking balls." And Cerrano misses those by two feet.

And that goes on the whole movie. Like he tries to use voodoo to fix it because he's supposed to be from some country with voodoo. I don't know where that is, but I know he's supposed to not be Christian. He says, "Jesus, I like him very much, but he no help with curveball," which isn't something you'd really say if you were Christian.

Anyway, the other teams figure it out, and they show him striking out again and again on curveballs. I never thought too much about it before. It just seemed funny. I mean, curveballs are hard to hit, but he's supposed to be a major leaguer.

But now I'm thinking about it a lot and paying attention every time he's at the plate. Because it's so basic: They've got him figured out. It could be curveballs or anything else. It could be inside pitches.

So I'm watching Cerrano swing two feet over the top of a slow hanging curve and thinking: That's me. That's me right there on the screen. When he says, "Bats, they are sick," I hear "Jack, he is sick." When he says,

"Curveball, bats are afraid," I hear "Inside pitch, Jack is afraid."

And it might as well be on TV, too. It might as well be in a movie that everyone on the team has seen. It might as well be because everyone who doesn't know already will know pretty soon: Jack can't hit inside pitches. Like I said, everybody watches everybody. If they pitch, you're an opponent, and if they don't, you're competition.

Everyone will know. Which means that's all I'll see. By Saturday, there's a good chance the Rockies will know, too. It's the same school, and people talk. And people watch. It's like with Dustin. No matter who we play, the first pitch he gets is always outside. I try to imagine that for a second.

The movie is just rolling along. It's one of the best parts, but I feel weak and panicky. Every at-bat would be like the last one. Everything would be hard and inside, locking me up. I'd just be standing there feeling scared and lame.

I get up and walk over to my window. There's a scuffed-up old baseball on the sill. I got a big hit with it in minors. I pick it up. It's heavy. You forget that. I can feel the hide where it's sort of torn up.

I toss it up in the air, and it smacks back down into my palm. It's heavy and hard and rough. It's like a big round rock.

It's so ridiculous. I just completely washed out at practice, but here I am holding a baseball. I look at the walls, covered with baseball posters, and the shelves, full of bobbleheads and baseball books.

I throw it up again, higher, almost to the ceiling. It smacks back down into my palm again, hard enough to sting. It's like a weapon.

Weapons are for wars, and I lost this one. Not just to Malfoy. He was only part of it. That's why it didn't make any sense to fight him. It wouldn't have made any difference. I lost to baseball, to the whole sport. To that big pitcher Saturday, who didn't even mean it. To Coach, who didn't, either. And to my good old buddy Meach, who did.

I don't know what I'll do without baseball. But I guess I'm going to find out. Here's the thing: That last at-bat was torture, straight up, and I just don't think I can do that again.

On TV, the Indians are about to win the big game, like they always do: Give him the heater, Ricky! I feel like throwing this baseball right through the screen.

Chapter

31

I have that nightmare again: faceless pitcher, feet stuck in cement. . . . I don't even get back to sleep, but at least that gives me plenty of time to think. Friday morning, I come downstairs wearing an ACE bandage on my left wrist.

"Whoa, whoa, whoa!" says Dad.

"What did you do?" says Mom. "Are you all right?"

They're both busy getting ready for work, but the sight of my lame one-handed wrap job has changed everything. They're like two birds sitting on their perch one second and flapping all around their cage the next.

Except you don't have to lie to birds.

"Yeah," I say, trying to sound upset. Upset but brave, which is the ridiculous part. "Yeah, you know, in practice yesterday."

The less I say the better, not just because it means the

less I can forget and get wrong later, but because I feel awful saying it.

"No, sport, we don't know," Dad says, looking at Mom.

"Yeah, yesterday, I just . . ."

They're still watching, waiting.

". . . in the field," I offer.

Still watching.

I exhale. "Yeah, I dove for a liner. Total dying duck . . . shouldn't have done it . . . glove kind of turned over on me . . ."

By the time I reach that last one they're coming out almost as questions: Glove kind of turned over on me?

"OK," says Dad, meaning either I've said enough or I've said too much, and he knows I'm lying.

How can he think I'm lying, I think, trying to muster some outrage. Can't he see the bandage? I'm just trying to think like I would if this was real. Which I really, really wish it was.

"Do we?" my mom begins, and then she seems to make up her mind. "We're going to the hospital."

Dad looks over at her. "Really?" he says, but his expression says: I'll barely make it to work on time as it is.

"I don't care, Stephen," she says. "Our son is hurt."

And it isn't an answer as much as a minefield. First of all, Mom only uses Dad's real name when she's serious. Like, seriously serious. Usually it's honey or something like that. And if she does use his name, it's usually Stevie.

But he got the full Stephen this time. And then the way she said *our son*, like he might have forgotten . . .

"It's nothing," I start, trying to back things down. "I mean it's not nothing, but . . ."

I trip over the double negative and stop, trying to figure out what I just said.

"Seemed to be handling that Big Mac pretty good last night," Dad says, looking at me. Is it getting hot in here?

"I'm right-handed?" I offer lamely.

Dad frowns.

"It stiffened up overnight!" I blurt out, speaking as fast as I think. Maybe faster.

His expression turns more neutral. That does happen.

I push the elastic bandage out toward him, like Nax extending a hurt paw.

"It does look a little swollen," says Mom.

That would be the sweatband I put under there.

"What does Coach say?" Dad says finally.

"Well, Coach Meacham says I probably just need a few days."

This is my big move, my checkmate-I-win move. Because Coach Meacham is on the volunteer fire department, so he has first-aid training. I think he's even "certified" or something. Anyway, it seems to work.

"So, no doctor?" Mom says.

I shake my head no, as firmly as possible. Can you imagine, Dr. Redick, standing there with his long white coat on? Unwrapping the bandage, ready to add yet another injury to my long list of bruises, cuts, and sprains, and finding a slightly swollen . . . wristband? I wouldn't be the first person to die at that hospital, just the first person to die of embarrassment.

"A few days?" Dad says.

There's a long pause. Everyone is thinking it.

"The game's on Saturday."

"Yeah," I say, exhaling loudly. "Just supposed to see how it feels tomorrow morning."

"Well, let me get some ice for it," Mom says.

Just like that, they're back to their morning routine. I take my ice pack and a pack of Pop-Tarts in my "good" hand and head for the TV room. I can hear them still talking about it as I walk away.

"Guess that's why he was so upset last night," Dad is saying.

"You took him to McDonald's?"

I know it's horrible, but it's something I have to do. Because as bad as it felt to stand there at the plate yesterday, freaking out, basically peeing myself — and then getting drilled for my trouble. Well, that's how good it feels knowing that I won't have to do that again, in front of half the town, tomorrow.

And then there's the nightmare. I've had it twice already. I don't want to have it a third time — or a tenth.

And you might be thinking, well, why not just quit, then. And, whatever, give me a break. I've been playing for half my life. It's not the kind of thing you can do in one quick step. It's not like ripping off a Band-Aid, OK?

Nax comes up and nuzzles my leg. He's wiping his cruddy eye on my pants again but also hoping for some Pop-Tart. He tips his snout up and licks the bandage on my left hand.

"Ow," I say. "Careful, boy."

Great, I just lied to my dog.

Chapter 32

I finish taking off the ACE bandage just as the bus door opens in front of me. I feel like an undercover mummy. I stuff it into my open backpack as I climb the steps and turn to survey my seating options.

Of course, I end up sitting with the same guy.

"Hey, Zeb," I say, collapsing into the seat.

"Hey," he says.

We don't say anything for most of the ride. Neither of us wants to talk about the game for completely opposite reasons. He's afraid he'll give something away. What a joke.

The silence gets a little awkward after a while. We hit a monster pothole, same one we always hit, and Zeb goes, "Waa-ha!" He doesn't exactly say it to me, and it's not exactly a word, but it's something.

It feels like it's my turn, so I say, "Anyone ever call you Z?"

"No," he says. "Why?"

But I misunderstand.

"They call you Y?" I say.

He just looks at me, and then we both realize what happened and start laughing. The two boys in the seat in front of us turn around. They're younger, like fourth grade. "What's so funny?" says the bigger of the two.

"Ask Y!" I say, and we both lose it again.

The fourth graders just look at each other — like: Did we miss something? — and turn back around.

Zeb and I get serious when the bus turns up the hill toward school. For him, it's a game face. For me, it's something worse.

I try not to be too mopey around Andy. I feel worse than I have all week, but it's not his fault. I'm carrying around the ACE in my backpack all day, like a trophy for Loser of the Year. I have English last today, and we have a test on *The Island of Dr. Moreau*. I know I'm going to review those notes right before, so I put a sticky note at the top. "Remember AB," it says, so I'll remember to put the ACE bandage on again when I go home. It's code, in case anyone sneaks a look at my notes.

The island turned out to be a total nightmare. I mean, surprise, right? Pumping out half human, half animal monsters on a deserted island goes wrong? Whuh? Still, it doesn't seem like such a bad place to be right now. Put me on some island in the middle of the ocean. I'll take my chances with the Him-panzees and the hungry, hungry Her-pos.

Anyway, the test I'm pretty much ready for. It's getting to last period that's the tough part. Lunch is the worst. For the first time all year, I have to think hard about where to sit. Usually there's no question. But now I'm walking toward my normal spot, and I see a table full of starters. They're already talking a mile a minute, and I know what they're talking about.

A few tables over, there's half a dozen Rockies doing the same thing. Not like anyone could hear anything over all the noise in here at lunchtime, but both tables are leaning in, like they're swapping secrets. There are other tables across the caf doing the same thing.

If I sit down at my normal table, it's going to be a pity party. At the start of the season, we were all just hoping to start. Now, all of a sudden, I'm the only one of my friends who isn't a starter. Except Chester, I guess, but he's our best sub, so he might as well be one.

The table is packed today. There's space to squeeze in, but my usual spot is taken by Jackson. That's enough of an excuse for me. As I walk up, a few of them start to scoot over to make room. I shake my head no.

"I can't fit there," I say, even though it's pretty obvious I could. "Gonna grab an open spot. Have to cram for English."

They look at me with open mouths, maybe not hearing me or maybe just not believing it, trying to decide if it's another one of my lame jokes. Andy has his head up, trying to make eye contact. If he sees my eyes, he'll know I'm ducking them. I avoid looking directly at him. I just nod and keep walking.

It feels weird. It feels, I don't know . . . bad.

The cafeteria is dotted with kids who used to play, kids who dropped out in minors or didn't make the jump to majors. We call them washouts, and right now, I'm avoiding their eyes, too. There's an empty spot up ahead, a few kids I sort of know. It's not that big a school.

"Mind if I grab a seat?" I say to no one in particular.

No one in particular objects, so I drop my tray onto the table with a loud plastic *blonk!*

I look around and see button-up shirts, glasses, and two kids playing each other on matching handheld video games. I know where I am. I know what table this is. You do, too.

"To what do we owe this rare honor?" says Jared.

"All full up over there," I say, shrugging.

Jared looks over. He's not dumb.

I try again: "Gotta study."

You'd think they could at least get behind that.

"So how ya been?" he says, ignoring what I just said or just not believing it. In his world, I'm a jock, and jocks don't study.

In my world, everyone calls him Comic-book Guy, and no one talks to him. But my world is changing. I'm changing it.

I exhale loudly, but he acts like he doesn't notice. I realize everyone else at the table has stopped talking. Those two kids have paused their games.

"Ehh," I say. "I'll survive."

The talking starts up again. I want to look back. To see if Andy, Tim, Dustin, Chester, and Jackson are looking over here or if they're already back to leaning in and talking low about the game. I want to, but I don't.

Chapter

33

"How'd you do?" Andy says after last period.

He's talking about the test. We still haven't talked about lunch.

"I aced it," I say, and that's just the reminder I need. *Remember AB.*

"Thanks," I say.

"For what?"

"Nothing," I say.

We head to the buses.

"See you tomorrow!" he says.

I'm supposed to say something like "Yeah, gonna crush 'em!" but I just nod.

He probably thinks I'm just down about losing my spot, so he tries again. "You'll be in there by the third."

No I won't, I think, but I just nod again. We reach the point where we have to split up to go to our buses.

"See ya," I say.

"Yeah, OK," he says. And then, "We're gonna destroy 'em."

I nod again and head for my bus.

I consider calling out, "Mercy rule," just to make him happy, but I won't do it. He's my best friend, and I won't lie to him.

Chapter

34

Lying to my parents, on the other hand, I mean, that's different. It's not even really lying. It's like part of the game, right? Like stealing a base? OK, so maybe that's not exactly true, but don't even pretend you've never faked a fever or blamed the cat for breaking something or anything like that. Don't even pretend to pretend.

Still, I have to lay it on pretty thick, and I definitely don't feel good about it. I walk around all night with my carefully bandaged wristband.

"Let me take a look at it," says Mom.

"No!" I say, and then, "The school nurse taped it up underneath. Supposed to keep it taped until tomorrow."

I'm in so deep now, what does one more lie even matter?

"It's a wrap, hon," she says. "I can just unwrap it and

wrap it right back up after. It's not like we're sawing off a cast here."

"Yeah," I say, "but, I mean, all you'd see is tape, right?"

She gives me a long look and I walk away, hoping she won't call me back. She doesn't. The whole night is like that. I go up to my room early and kill about 10,000 video game soldiers in *Grunt Front*. I fire the grenade launcher until I'm out, then I overheat the machine gun and finally go down swinging with the knife.

The game is still on when I wake up in the morning. The screen saver is bouncing around from corner to corner.

I get up and turn it off, then go back and lie on top of the covers. The ACE is lying like a deflated snake on my desk, but I still have the wristband on, so I don't forget. It's easy to forget an injury when it's not real. Not much chance of that today.

If I do this, there's no going back. If I take this lie all the way and skip this game, that's it.

I roll around on the bed just to wake myself up so I can think. It's like, if I shake my brain hard enough, it will come up with the right decision. Like it's a Magic 8 Ball. I stop rolling around, but all my brain comes up with is: outlook unclear. I might even be a little dizzy.

I stand up again and walk over to my desk. I pinch the end of the ACE against my palm with my thumb and start wrapping. There are a few hours before the game. I can still take it off and tell my parents it feels good enough to play. I can even tell them that's why I'm not starting. It's a pretty good plan, except then I'd have to bat. Everyone bats at least once in Little League. And Coach might give me more. He'd think he was doing me a favor.

I can picture that at-bat. I can feel it in my stomach.

I keep wrapping until I'm done.

I walk all of twenty feet, close the door to the bathroom, and unwrap it all again for my shower.

"How's the wrist, sport?" Dad asks as soon as I walk into the kitchen.

I just look at him. How do I tell him I haven't decided yet?

I make a show of trying to flex it.

"Ehh," I say.

"Ehh?" he says, not satisfied.

"Little stiff," I say.

"Well, give it a bit."

"Yuh," I say, and pour myself some cereal.

Mom comes in, either to get something or because she heard me.

"Little stiff," Dad reports.

I look up and nod.

That's the thing about these big decisions: You can make them one little step at a time. An hour later, I'm ready to take a big one. "Not sure I'll be able to play today," I say. "Just don't think I can swing the bat."

And at least the second half of that is true.

"Well," says Dad, looking at his watch, "you got . . . maybe . . . fifty minutes before we leave."

And that's when I realize it: They plan to go to the game either way. I can't go to the game with this wrap on! The whole team knows I'm not hurt. I feel a big wave of panic roll in.

"Y'okay," I say, and push through the door out onto the lawn. It's only at the last second that I remember not to use my left hand.

Oh man oh man oh man. If I go to the game, I have to take the wrap off. But if I take the wrap off, I have to play. And I can't play. They'll be pitching me hard inside, hard inside. If I get hit again right now, I don't even know what will happen. And even if I don't, I'll just get embarrassed again up there. I'll get embarrassed, and I'll let the team down. What if there are runners on? What if we're behind? You can't just give up at-bats and expect to win.

I start to list it off:

I could get hit.

I could be humiliated.

I could cost my team the game.

My parents could talk to someone and find out I've been lying.

I kick the big tree out front and run through all the swears I know. It's a pretty good list.

And it's stupid, too, because, I mean, of course they'd want to go. I've never missed a game before. I've dragged myself to the field even if it was just to sit on the bench all game. I've shown up with colds, the flu, limps, bruises, and everything else short of a knife sticking out of my chest.

It's completely clear now. They plan to take me to the field, and they're probably like 90 percent sure I'll play anyway.

I look over my shoulder. Mom is watching me through the front window. I suck in air and look down quick at the ACE. It's fine, and I breathe out. I don't know why I thought it had come undone. I guess it's because everything else has.

Chapter 35

The panic passes after a few more kicks to the tree. Mom is probably still watching, but it doesn't matter. This is what I'd be doing anyway. This tree takes a beating sometimes.

The solution falls right in front of me like I shook loose an acorn. I'll just have to tell them. No need to over-think this: I'll just tell them I don't want to go.

And that's what I do. I take a few fake practice swings in the yard and then storm into the house. "Can't do it," I announce to the empty living room. "Wrist is really . . . can't swing . . . hurts."

It's just as well they weren't there for that one. I take a deep breath and try again in the kitchen. This time, I have an audience. I tell them I can't play and wait for it.

"Well, I guess we don't have to get there so early," says Dad.

"Sure you don't want to see the doctor?" says Mom.

"No, I don't want to go," I say.

"All right," says Mom. "But I want to take a look at it once the tape is off."

It's like every problem turns into two problems with this. I take a breath. I just have to deal with one at a time.

"To the game, I mean," I say. "I don't want to go to the game."

"You always go to the game, sport," says Dad.

"I think, you know, hon, I think we want to go to the game," says Mom. "And I think you should come, too."

I'm sort of caught in the cross fire, but I dig in my heels. I'm like Nax trying to avoid going to the vet's, if Nax could talk. It's basically just: I don't wanna go, I don't wanna go, I don't wanna go. I don't want to go and sit in the bleachers.

All of that is true, which makes it easier.

I do everything short of chaining myself to a water pipe. Dad is smart, though. I mean, Mom and Dad are both smart, but Dad is suspicious.

"This doesn't, uh . . ." Dad starts. "This doesn't have anything to do with last week?"

It stings, especially because it's true.

"No," I say. "Nuh-uh. Course not."

So one more lie creeps in there. Then I start all over again, like a recording: I don't wanna go, I don't wanna go, I don't wanna go. I don't want to go and sit in the bleachers.

Finally, I must say something that clicks with Dad. He turns to Mom and says, "He doesn't want to sit and watch. He's a competitor."

That stings, too, and *not* because it's true. All I can tell myself is: I used to be.

"He's just upset," Mom says finally. She says it to Dad, but she's looking at me. Or maybe she's talking to me and she means that Dad's upset, which he is.

"Me, too," I say, and I head upstairs.

I want to scream or break something or at least, you know, kill a bunch of soldiers in *Grunt Front*. But I have one more thing to do first. I get out the team contact list and call Coach's cell phone.

It goes to voice mail, like I knew it would this close to a game. Just hearing his voice for three seconds on the message makes me feel like I'm in trouble. But it also reminds me of those at-bats, of him saying "pinch-runner," and I guess that gives me what I need to get it done.

I keep it vague: "Family emergency . . . Pretty bad . . . Sorry . . ." If he needs more, he can ask. And he won't really care about my excuse after this because, I mean, that's it, right? I have to quit now. How do you go back after something like this? I guess this is what I wanted. I guess, because it's what I just did.

I put the list back in the drawer without looking at it. I don't want to see the names. Then I just lie down on the bed, completely motionless. I look up at the ceiling, and my face feels hot enough to melt the paint above me.

After a while, I look over at my alarm clock. They're warming up now. A little while later, I look again: must be the first inning, maybe the second. I can picture the infield, all the way around: Jackson at first, Tim at second, Katie at short, and Andy at third. Behind them, looking in, it's Geoff.

I just lie there until I'm pretty sure the game is over. I don't get to do anything while they're playing. Once enough time has passed, I get up and kill some soldiers.

By the time I clear the next level, I already have three e-mails. I check my cell, which is on silent: two texts and a voice mail. I can't answer them yet. But I'll have to do it soon. Otherwise, they'll start calling the house.

I start the next level, and I'm running from tanks and looking for an RPG in the rubble. I have got to stop using up all my grenades so quickly, but I'll have plenty of time to work on that.

In the afternoon, I send seven short texts: "Sorry! Fam. emergency!!!" times six, and "Call U tomorrow!!!" to Andy.

That night I go to bed earlier than I have in years. Nax climbs aboard and curls up at the foot of my bed. He's not supposed to, but I let him. He knows something is wrong.

I lie there and tell him the whole thing. It's too early to sleep, anyway. I talk low, but dogs have superhearing, right?

I'm talking for a long time. Whenever I stop, Nax looks back at me and lets out a little woof. He thinks it's a game, a talking game. And so I end up telling him everything, about baseballs and bad dreams and ACE bandages. Hope he's not wearing a wire.

Finally, I tell him how I have to quit now, because I let everyone down and I'm useless and told different stories to different people, anyway. I don't say how I painted myself into this corner because I'm still so afraid of the ball that I just want out.

"It's really the only thing I have left," I tell my dog. "Stick a fork in me."

It's quiet when I finish, then Nax lets out one more soft bark. He thinks we're still playing the game. *Ruff*, he says.

I scratch his head.

"You got that right," I say.

Chapter

36

It's Sunday night and I'm thinking, How do you do it? What are the mechanics of quitting your team? It's so easy on TV. There's an announcement, a press conference. The athlete speaks for a few minutes and cries a little at the end. That's the part that goes on ESPN: some guy with gray in his hair tearing up in front of two dozen microphones.

But no one's going to hold a press conference for me. I'm going to have to tell people one at a time. The ACE is off, but I've wrapped my wrist up in two layers of white athletic tape, the stuff that was supposed to be under there the whole time anyway.

I walk past Mom and Dad in the living room. They're sitting on the couch. The TV is on, there are snacks set out, and Dad has a beer. I hear the announcer's voice: "Sunday Night Game of the Week." I can still do that. I can still watch. The players can't look through the TV, shake their heads in disgust, and turn their backs on me. I mean, we've got HD, but it's not *that* good.

I look at Mom and Dad. There's a spot for me on the couch, like always. But this time, it's right in between them. It's a bad sign. I sit down in between my parents.

"Who's playing?" I say.

They don't answer right away. I just look and see for myself. There's a saying, something Dad used to say to me when I asked questions like that. I just go ahead and say it for him. "If you'd look with your eyes and not with your mouth, maybe you'd find out."

"Yep," says Dad.

"Yep," says Mom.

"Yep," I say.

It's the Yankees versus the Indians. It makes me think of *Major League* and all those funny lines, like "Couldn't cut it in the Mexican League." I'm going to have a T-shirt made up that says that.

We don't divide up into teams this time. There's no Brew Crew versus Los Dodgeros. We all root against the Yankees.

I need to tell them, but there's just no way I can do it right now, sitting in between them on the couch, watching this game. What am I supposed to say: "Didn't really look like he ran out that fly ball. Speaking of quitting on your team . . ."?

Anyway, the Yankees jump on the Tribe early. It's a total blowout by the sixth, and I decide to go upstairs.

"Homework," I say.

I wait for them to object, but they don't. They know I lied to them. They figured it out or maybe they talked to someone. I think about the three or four times the phone rang today. I get off the couch and Dad does, too.

"I'm getting another beer," he says.

"Don't, Stephen," says Mom, but he does.

Upstairs, I close the door to my room. I try to do my homework. I make stacks out of my books and decide what to do first.

None of it looks very good. Normally, I'd start with English, but our new assignment for English is poetry. I don't want to read any poems right now.

I don't think I can concentrate enough for math. I pick up my history book and flip through it. That's about as much as I get done. I'll do as much as I can tomorrow, I tell myself. It seems like a good morning to be bent over a book, anyway. A good morning to be reading and doing problems and not, you know, talking.

That reminds me: I still haven't called Andy. I pick up my phone. I just look at that, too.

Chapter

37

And then I catch a break.

It's been so long since I've seen one, I barely recognize it. I'm on the bus Monday morning, sort of on autopilot. The torn-off tape wrap is stuffed in my backpack, even though Saturday morning seems like a million years ago already.

Zeb is already sitting with someone, and I don't want to sit with him anyway. I still don't know who won the game, and if it was the Rockies, I don't want to find out from him. I don't want to find that out from anyone.

So I'm sitting with a spastic fourth grader, who is, honest to God, burping loudly. I expect him to vomit on me before we make it to school, and it's like, yep, this is my life.

And then a kid named Morgan one seat up turns around and looks at me.

"Where were you?" he says.

Morgan is a year below me but a year ahead of Sir Burps-a-lot here, so it's a step up. He doesn't play much — he's like a physical extension of the bench — but he never misses a practice.

"Family emergency," I say. He doesn't look satisfied with that, which he shouldn't, because it's lame. But he can't call me on it because he's younger. He's about to turn around. I take a deep breath and do what my dad would call "biting the bullet." You know: getting it over with.

"How'd it go?" I say.

"What?" he says.

"The game? We win?"

"Yeah, yeah," he says. "Barely."

He turns around to see where Zeb and those guys are. Then he turns back. He isn't whispering, because the rumble of the bus is too loud for that, but he's, you know, bus-whispering.

"I don't think the Rox are that good this year," he continues, making a goofy face to show how non-good he thinks they are. "I mean, even I got a hit, right?"

I'm about to congratulate him, but he's still talking.

"But it was" — he looks around again — "Meacham. Kurt, not Coach."

He means Malfoy, but younger kids can't call him that.

"What about him?"

Morgan looks around again, so I can tell whatever it is must be really good.

I look over at the fourth grader. He's picking his nose.

"Hey, booger," I say, and nod toward Morgan. "Swap seats."

Booger looks at me for a second, a small boulder of snot still impaled on his index finger. I look him in the eye.

"OK," he says.

He's scared of me. I'm going to miss being a jock.

He wipes the snot on his jeans and scoots by. I try not to let any part of him touch me. Then I shove over toward the window, and Morgan lands on the end of the seat.

"Siddown back there!" calls the bus driver, but we're already, you know, sidding.

"OK, so . . ." I say.

Morgan leans in: "OK, OK. He got slammed!"

"Malfoy?" I say.

"Yeah," he hesitates, "Malfoy." Then he repeats it, "Malfoy."

"Like how, 'slammed'?" I say.

"Didn't make it out of the third!"

"Seriously?"

"Seriously! Gave up, like" — he starts ticking off with his fingers — "five runs!"

And the way he says that, I can just tell: "You don't like him either."

"Nah," he says. You can tell there's more to that story, but I'm still stuck on the last part. I was right! I mean, I was kind of joking when I said it, when Malfoy overheard me, but I was still right!

"Who'd Coach bring in?" I say, getting greedy.

"Dustin," he says.

OK, so I wasn't right about that part.

"But that's not it. That's not, like, even the main thing!"

"What? What's the main thing?"

"Kurt — Malfoy — he lost it!"

"Seriously?"

"Seriously!"

"Lost it how?"

"He hit two batters! Both late! You know what I mean? I mean . . ." But I know what he means.

"In the third?"

"Yeah! We're already down five to zippo, right? So the last thing we need is more base runners, but he drills two guys, one after the other. And the first guy, OK, maybe it's an accident — even though he hit a triple off him in the first. But the second? Coach had to go get him before it got out of hand. But it almost did anyway."

"Whoa!" I say, because there are so many things shooting through my mind right now. There's fear because, you know, I've been there. Boy, have I. But there's also satisfaction because I was right, and a half-dozen other things.

I guess I get lost in space for a while because, next thing I know, Morgan is going, "Jack? Jack?"

"Yeah," I say, snapping out of it.

Neither of us says anything for a few seconds.

"Should I go back to my seat?" he says.

"What? No," I say. "So, we're down five-nothing, runners on, and Coach brings in Dustin?"

"Yeah, yeah," says Morgan. "You know, he's got a pretty good fastball, so . . ."

And he goes from there, telling me how Dustin got out of the jam and the team climbed out of a 5–0 hole.

As he's talking, I realize that I've just been let off the hook. Or at least I've been bumped up to the tip where I might be able to wriggle off. Kids are going to be talking about baseball all day, but they won't be talking about me. Let's just be honest here: A family emergency, even a real one, isn't half as interesting as a full-fledged pitching meltdown.

Malfoy . . . Huh . . . looks like my former friend did me one last favor after all.

This is the week I was going to have to either quit the team or get back into the batter's box. And this is the day I was going to have to quit or lie to the face of everyone I know. Now I'm thinking, I don't have to quit today.

And then it occurs to me as I'm filing down the aisle of the bus, heading for the door. Morgan is still chattering behind me, and Zeb is avoiding my eyes, and it just pops in there: Do I even have to quit at all?

Part III
RALLY CAP

Chapter

38

I take a few half steps toward Andy in the hallway, and he just launches himself and delivers this flying UFC Superman punch to my left arm.

"Ehahohaaaaa," I say. It's not a word as much as just air escaping from my lungs, because I'm trying not to say *ow*, but it really hurts.

"Where were you, dingus?" he blurts.

I had something prepared to say to him, but he hit my arm so hard he knocked it out of my head.

"Well, I had a, like there was this family sort of emergency except that, OK, the emergency was really basically me, and it's not like I was going to start anyway, and then also because —" He raises his hand to punch me again and I shut up and hold up my right arm. I put my palm out in a stop sign, like: *no más*.

"OK, whatever, dingus," he says, and I just know I'm going to be dingus all day now. "We'll talk about that later, and we will, because you are in serious trouble, seriously."

And then here it comes.

"But did you hear? Can you believe it? Malfoy! King Turd really outdid himself this time!" And then he launches into his own version of how it all went down.

It's like that all morning. It's all over the school. At least with the people I know. My "family emergency" comes up a few times, but when it does, "How 'bout Malfoy?" is my Get Out of Jail Free card.

I mix it up a little, just so its magic powers won't wear off. "So the first guy hit a triple off him? What about the second guy?" Or "Man, Dustin came up big, huh?" Or just "What was the final score again?" because, of course, that leads to the same place. And I get more info that way, anyway.

And then I get to math and Ms. Part hands me back my test. She hands it back front side up, so I know it's either really good and she thinks I should be proud or it's really bad and she thinks I should study harder. I see some flashes of red ink here and there, so I'm thinking, you know, uh-oh.

It was a hard test, too, because there were a lot of fractions and negative numbers and all that tricky stuff. I look at the top, the only red ink that counts, and it's a 92. I got an A! Or, OK, an A-, but still.

I tip it so Andy can see, and he makes a whistling shape with his lips and nods his head, like: Pretty good, Einstein.

So I'm feeling pretty good about that. And I catch sight of Malfoy a few times, slinking between classes, and I feel pretty good about that, too. And before you know it, it's time for lunch. I thought this was going to be the worst day ever, but when I get to the table, Andy is saving me a seat.

I look over at Jared and those guys. They're looking over, but it's not like they're surprised when I sit down next to Andy. I think we're going to talk some more about Malfoy, but I'm wrong.

"Where were you, jerk-weed?" says Jackson.

"Yeah, 'family emergency,' my bulbous behind," says Tim.

I look over at the other table. There's a spot open by Jared, but I'd never make it. I'd get cut down in the cross fire before I even finished standing up.

"Uh," I say.

"Uhhhhhh," Jackson says, his eyes going panicky, imitating mine.

"Shut up," I say. "This is serious."

Though I don't know what it is, or exactly why it's serious. I haven't really worked out my cover story. This is the part where I was going to let them know I was quitting. This is the part where I was going to be sitting at the other table. This is the part where everything but this was going to happen.

But there's nothing I can do about it now. This is the part where the momentum of one good morning runs me straight into a brick wall.

"Yeah, what's so serious?" Dustin says. "You being a wuss?"

"Shut up," I say again. It's the one thing you can always say when you can't think of what to say, but I can't say it all lunch. They're not letting this go.

"Mommy, I don't want to go to the game," says Jackson.

"Don't let the big, bad baseball hit me again, Mommy," says Dustin.

I stare at him. I glare at him. How could he know? I mean, he was the catcher, he was right there, but still. I look at him looking at me: It was a guess. Now he's watching my reaction, seeing if it's true. And I'm giving him everything he needs.

I look over at Andy. He always bails me out, but he's not giving me a break this time.

"Yeah," he says. "Where were you?"

I'm thinking that this is the part where I quit after all. Those are the only words I have rehearsed, the only ones I can think of right now. And I don't want to lie to all of my friends. I'd feel bad about it, and I'd mess it up. I feel cornered. They'll grill me, and it will fall apart and it will be even worse. I'll be the kid who lied and then quit anyway. And they'll be my ex-friends, like Malfoy.

I think about it again: standing in the box with the ball coming at me. I think about the game, the practice, the nightmares. I need that fear now to make me do it, to make me follow through.

"Where were you?" Andy says again, and I want to say: I HEARD YOU THE FIRST TIME! And then I hear the rest of the sentence: ". . . they have the funeral already?"

Now everyone is looking at him, me included. What is he talking about?

"It's a bummer, man," he says, shrugging his shoulders. "I really liked your uncle."

Now they're looking from him to me. I shrug my shoulders, look down, do all the things Andy just did.

"No," I say. I pause, and an amazing thing happens: The words just float up and out of me.

"No," I say again. I look up into their eyes. "It was too sudden. Family's still got to, you know, get things in order. Make all the arrangements."

I don't know much about funerals, but I know those are words people use.

"Oh, man," says Jackson. "Sorry about that."

"Yeah," says Dustin. "My bad."

I look over at Andy, and I try so, so hard not to smile.

Chapter 39

I'm at home, killing soldiers. I'm not as angry this time, not using up all my ammo first thing. I'm playing slow and smart. Sometimes it helps me to think, and I have a lot to think about.

There are tanks coming up behind me, but they're on my side. As they open fire, I make a break across an open field.

"Tanks a lot," I say under my breath as I reach a foxhole.

It reminds me of lunch. Covering fire, that's what that was. That's what Andy gave me. He didn't win the battle for me or make it all go away, but he bought me some time. He put his own neck on the line, and he gave me some cover when I needed it.

So what do I do with it? That's the question. My army

guy is crouched down behind a brick wall now, and he can go left or right. I've got two choices, too. That's what I've got to think about.

I turn off the game and look around. Man, my room is a mess. It looks like bombs have gone off in here. I guess I've been a little out of it. I guess I've been a little out of everything.

I hear a muffled *woof!* from somewhere. "Nax?" I say, because it seems like he might be buried under one of the piles in here. There's no response, so I start tossing rumpled clothes into the corner. The socks I throw onto the bed, hoping to match them into pairs. Then I get a whiff of a mismatched gray tube sock and reconsider putting them on my bed.

From there, everything goes into the hamper. I hold my breath as I lift the lid, but it takes too long to cram all the new stuff inside, and I take a deep gasping breath that makes my eyes water.

After that, I walk around putting other stuff away: DVDs, books, random junk. Half an hour later, the room is starting to look halfway civilized. I look around to see what else needs to be done, and that's when I see the new cards Dad got me.

The pile has tipped over on the edge of my desk, and a few of the cards are even on the floor next to it. I walk over and pick those up first, hoping they aren't anything good. Let me just put it this way: Nothing that's been on my floor this week will ever be described as mint condition again. Potentially toxic is more like it.

Luckily, the floor cards are all doubles or so-so players. I brush them off and then go to my closet for a box to put them in. I don't have a real light in there, just one of those battery-powered things with sticky tape on the back. I punch the plastic front and it lights up.

On the shelf above my good shirts, I have all the cards, going all the way back. The years are written on the front of the boxes, but you could almost tell when they're from just by the handwriting. The first years are just a little kid's scrawl. The first one is actually in crayon.

I don't know why I do it, but I start taking them all down. I walk them over to the bed in two armfuls. I put them down on the side that isn't contaminated by socks and start to go through them.

Every year is the same: Most of the cards are lined up in neat rows, alphabetical by team. But the best cards are in little plastic sleeves at the front. I start going through those.

I really do have some good cards. None of these are my dad's Cal Ripken card, but, I mean, his Ripken card probably wasn't such a big deal when he first got it. Maybe one of these cards I'm flipping through right now will be like that one day. And I'm thinking something else, too. I'm thinking about when I got them.

The box I'm going through now, I got that in second grade. I remember I was all grimy from practice, and Dad made me go wash up before he'd let me open the cards. I didn't really understand at the time. Second grade, you know?

This next box is from third grade, and by then I understood. He gave these to me after one of our games got rained out. I was sulking on the couch, and it was just what I needed. Every time I saw a player I recognized, I thought it was a treasure, and by the end I was bouncing off the couch. That's the year he started giving me the little plastic sleeves to put the best ones in.

So I'm just flipping through, and of course I've got more cards in the sleeves that year than any other. It's so dumb, but it's like I put half the cards in them. I sort of smile because, I mean, some of these cards are total junk! Yeah, I'm thinking, better protect *this* one.

I'm holding a rookie card for some guy who's not even in the majors anymore: Chuck Wagner; position: 1B; nickname: The Wagon. A drop of water splashes onto the edge of the plastic. That's when I realize I might be smiling a little, but I'm crying, too.

I look up, and the first thing I see is the line of baseball bobbleheads on my bookshelf. They're looking right at me with their big, stupid heads.

"What are you looking at?" I say, but I can't help but let out a little laugh.

They're looking at some kid crying onto a three-year-old card that belongs in a trash can instead of a plastic sleeve. They're looking at a kid who's been collecting these things since he could walk, who's been through each of these boxes two dozen times.

I look above the bobbleheads, at the row of baseballs. They've got little notes written on them in magic marker, just some reason why I kept each one and the date. I don't need to read the notes anymore. I know what they say. There's "first game" and "first homer" and "first win," from back when I thought I might be a pitcher. They go all the way up to the second-to-last game last season and a game-winning double I hit.

I look to the right of the shelf, at the big poster from the Baseball Hall of Fame and Museum in Cooperstown, New York. I broke a tooth on some candy Mom bought me in one of the gift shops. It doesn't mean I didn't finish the box. Or that it wasn't one of the best days of my life.

I draw my arm across my eyes and suck the snot back down. I stick the card in my back pocket and stand up.

Nax is trotting down the hallway as I leave my room. He doesn't know where I'm going, but he decides to follow me. As I start down the stairs, I can hear the TV in the living room, and I march straight toward it. Mom and Dad are sitting on opposite sides of the couch, and they look up when I enter the room.

"Dad," I say. "How late do you think the batting cages are open?"

Chapter

40

"You sure your wrist is OK for this?" Dad says as he drops me off for practice on Tuesday. He doesn't usually drop me off, but he is working from home again. His office calls them flex days, and they're to save on commuting costs because a lot of people drive a long way to get there. I wish we had flex days at school.

"What?" I say.

I remember, and I'm about to start digging myself out of the hole I just fell into, but when I look over, he has a half smile on his face.

"Yeah," I say. I can't help but smile, too. I want to ask him how long he's known, if he bought my story for even a second. But I don't. This is one of those things you don't talk about. He knows, and I know he knows. That's enough. I still lied to my parents. Boy, did I. Best to let a thing like that drop.

"Fit as a fiddle," I say as I open the door. I know he likes that one, so it's like my way of saying thanks.

And then I make my way across the field, and all I have to deal with is the team I let down on Saturday. I feel nervous and kind of weirdly shy. I need a baseball, like, now.

"Toss it here," I say.

"Who? What? Me?" says Morgan.

"No, your mother," I say, and OK, maybe it's cheating to warm up with a fifth grader instead of Dustin, who's right behind him. I'm just not up to the team captain today, and Andy's not here yet.

Morgan throws me the ball, and we spread out for some long toss. He doesn't talk much, which is fine with me. I keep an eye on Coach the whole time. As I do, I see other eyes watching me.

Finally, Coach finishes taping up Tim's ankle. Tim is a big believer in the power of tape, and he must've gotten dinged up in the game.

Coach stands up and heads toward the field. His eyes lock on me right away.

"Hold it," I say, tossing the ball to Morgan. I swallow some spit and head toward my death. I'm trying to figure out what to say, or at least how to start: "Listen, Coach" or "OK, so the thing is . . ." But I don't even get the chance.

When he's still six feet away from me, he says, "You ready, Mogens?"

"Yeah," I manage.

"Good," he says, and keeps walking.

That's it? It doesn't make any sense. I just got a free pass from my dad and my coach, not ten minutes apart. And then I realize: He knows, too. Not about the tape and the excuses and all that, but he knows I skipped the game, and he knows why.

I remember the last thing he said to me: "It's been a pretty rough stretch for you; better catch a breather." I just thought he was talking about starting the game on the bench. That's what everyone thought. But now, I mean, it's almost like he knew.

I start to turn around. Some breather, I'm thinking. And that's when Andy punches me in the arm again. "Hey, dingus," he says.

"Aaaaaa," I say. "Same spot."

"Got a ball?" he says.

I point to Morgan, who's standing there watching us.

Andy gives me a look, like: Why are you warming up with this kid?

I give him a shrug, like: Whatever, he's cool.

Then Andy holds up his glove. "Throw me the ball, little dingus," he calls to Morgan.

A few minutes later, practice starts. Practice starts, and I'm still on the team. I'm not a starter anymore, but I mean, that's what I'm here for, right? "Three of you thrown out on the bases, two at the plate," Coach is saying. "I have never been so sick in my entire life. Never before has the game of baseball filled me with such a powerful urge to puke my guts out. To puke my *consider- able* guts out."

It's hard not to smile when Coach says things like that, but he would go ballistic if any of us smiled right now, so we bite our lips and do our best.

"I have no idea how we won that game," he continues. "But we won't win another one with base-running like that. What we need is a dictionary. Does anyone have a dictionary so we can look up the word *slide*?"

I know what's coming. I have never, in all my time on a baseball field — in all my *considerable* time on a base- ball field — been so happy to do the lawsuit drill.

I'm going to have to bat today. I know that. I'm just glad I don't have to start with it. I sprint over to get near the front of the line. I'm right behind Katie. I swear it's a coincidence, mostly. I pull my hat down low so no one can see where my eyes are. There are all kinds of reasons to be glad I'm still on the team.

Then I reach down and button the back pocket of my practice pants. I'm going to be sliding, and I wouldn't want the card to come out, even if it is junk.

Chapter

41

So, to give you an idea of how I'm doing, I'm trying to make myself feel better by thinking about that recurring nightmare. At least you can move your feet this time, I tell myself. Then I look up and see Coach going into his windup.

I take a deep breath, but that's all the preparation I get done before the pitch is on the way. For a second, I think I'm freaking out again, just being paranoid and overreacting. But I'm not: Coach really is pitching me inside.

I manage not to dive backward or anything like that, and I take the pitch. I tell myself that it was a ball, but that's stupid because this is batting practice. The emphasis is on the first word.

I take another breath. Of course he's pitching me inside. Because that's what I need to hit. That's what

I need to show him. I step back in. Fine, I think, pitch me inside. I'll stick out my butt, and you can hit a former major leaguer in a protective practice sleeve. Chuck "The Wagon" Wagner isn't mint condition anymore, anyway.

That loosens me up a bit. The next pitch comes in, inside half, and I put a swing on it. I'm a little late and foul it down the first-base line. But it feels good, just that contact, the force of the bat hitting the ball going through my hands and up my arms. You can get so caught up with the idea of the ball hitting you that you forget that you're supposed to hit it. I think that's a little funny, too.

I step out. I can see that Coach is ready to start that little mini windup that he uses to deliver his lollipop pitches, and I know I'll probably get yelled at for this, but I hold up my hand.

Coach looks at the stop sign, and I guess maybe he doesn't know what to make of it. He doesn't go into his windup, though. That's important, because there's something I have to do.

First, I sort of dig my front foot in. I twist my toes into the dirt a few times, then I settle my weight onto my back foot. They always say: Sit down on the back leg. So that's what I do. Next, I take four swings, two fast and two slow.

"All right, Garciaparra!" Coach shouts. "Let's go!"

I intend to. I'm sick of this.

The pitch comes in. I'm not surprised when it's on the inside half of the plate. In fact, I'm counting on it. I start my swing early.

My mind is screaming to get away from the ball, and I'm still thinking of that nightmare. But I don't care. This is a meatball pitch on the inside half, and I know it's coming. I turn on it like I've always turned on pitches like this.

I feel the contact. The vibration shoots up my arms and goes right down to my feet. It's not that bad, stinging contact, either. It's the sweet, clean kind. I send a screamer down the third-base line that nearly takes Andy's head off.

"There you go!" shouts Coach. "Base hit!"

Andy is looking in his glove to see if he has it, but he doesn't.

I dig in for the next pitch. I'd like to say it's a homer, but it isn't. It's on the outside corner, and I get under it and lift a can of corn to right. I manage a few more liners before my turn is over, though. It's just BP, but it's something.

Coach calls Geoff in for his turn at the plate, and I grab my glove and head out to left. I don't read too much into it. Left field is still Geoff's. A few line drives aren't going to change that. It's a start, though.

"Tryin' to kill me?" Andy says as I run past him.

He's talking about the line drive. I can't think of anything clever to say, so I just smile. It's a full smile, teeth and everything. It's the first one in a long time, and it feels good.

Chapter

42

After school on Wednesday, Andy and I are riding our sixth-grade cars downtown. My sixth-grade car is a Huffy, and his is a Schwinn.

"Wanna jump it?" Andy says, nodding toward a lump of dark brown dirt.

We're riding along the stretch of pavement behind the supermarket. It's somewhere between a driveway, an alley, and an actual road. It's where the delivery trucks pull up, but there are none here now. The market sells potted plants, and it looks like maybe someone dumped some out or ran some over or something.

"OK," I say. I start pumping harder and stand up in my seat to get more power. I sit down right before I hit the lump and lift up on the handlebars to help with the jump.

It doesn't matter. The dirt isn't hard enough, and my wheels just cut ruts in it as they roll over. I fishtail a little at the end, but I don't go down.

"Lame," says Andy.

"Lame," I say, and we pedal on into the parking lot.

Andy dodges a car as it backs out of a parking space.

"Jerk!" he yells. Then he turns to me: "They didn't even signal."

You don't have to signal when you back up. I mean, there is no backup signal on a car. "Jerk," I say, anyway, because it's not worth pointing that out.

I feel like a dork with this helmet on, and I bet Andy does, too. But we have to wear them here. (A) It's the dumb law, and (B) there are too many people downtown we know, and they'd tell our folks. So it's like we're legally obligated to look like dorks. All we can do about it is call people jerks and attempt to jump over anything in our way.

We hop the curb onto the sidewalk and pedal on, looking for the next thing. Then we spend another half hour or so just tooling around downtown before we start hitting the same roads and alleys and sidewalks for the second and third time.

Behold downtown Tall Pines! There's just not that much to it.

"Pharmacy?" I say.

"Yeah, OK," says Andy.

We coast to a slow, thumping stop in the bike rack in front of the Tall Pines Family Pharmacy. Then we get off, take off our dorky helmets, and fasten our dorky bike locks.

"Your hair is deeply disturbing," I say to Andy.

"You got a little helmet head going on yourself," he says.

I smooth mine down, and he pushes his up into a faux hawk.

"Are you going in like that?" I say as we push through the door.

"Why not?" he says, but when I look back I see him smashing it back down onto his head.

We walk over to the magazine rack to check out the comic books and stuff. I realize I'm a little nervous, and it's not because this month's comics are in. I still haven't really told Andy about, you know, everything. It's something I have to do. He covered for me, and, I mean, I think he sort of knows anyway. Not telling him would make me a jerk, a real one, so I've got to bite the bullet and do it. If I don't do it soon, he'll go ahead and ask. And just him having to ask will make me at least half a jerk.

He holds up *Maxim* magazine so I can see the woman on the cover.

"So . . ." he says. "You heard anything about Campbeltown?"

That's who we're playing next. Campbeltown is a section of Tall Pines, and definitely not the main section, either. They have their own little school and their own team, though. You'd think they wouldn't be that good, because there aren't as many kids. The ones they have are big, though, like big farm kids.

"I don't know," I say. "They kind of took it to us last year."

"Yeah, but J.P. wasn't pitching," says Andy.

"Yep, and I don't know if those two really big kids are still on the team."

"At least one of them must be too old by now," he says.

"Yeah," I say, "the bigger one."

"Can't argue with that logic," he says.

"Hopefully they're both gone."

"Yep. Why weren't you at the game Saturday?" he says.

I carefully put back the magazine I'm holding. I don't say anything right away, and neither does he.

"Because I'm a jerk."

"True," he says. "Still doesn't explain it."

"Well," I say. "You remember the week before?"

"Yep," he says.

We aren't looking at each other. We just keep picking up magazines and comic books and putting them back.

"When I got hit in the head?"

"Not like it's a vital organ for you, but yeah."

"And then I got drilled by jerk-butt?"

"Yep."

"Well, I had enough of getting beat up with the stupid ball."

"I played four innings," he says. "No one hit me."

"Yeah, well, thing is," I say.

"Yeah, what's the thing?" he says.

"I was scared. Like seriously scared. Like I've been having nightmares."

And now I've said it and I'm embarrassed and relieved and worried about what he's going to say and whether he's going to tell anyone. He doesn't say anything right away, which doesn't help. He picks up another magazine and flips it open. He looks at one picture, then closes it and puts it back.

"Everyone's a little scared of the ball sometimes," he says. This time, he looks over.

I look over, too. "Yeah, but I was, like, a lot afraid of the ball, all the time."

He looks back at the magazines and raises his hand to the rack. But then he reconsiders and drops it.

"Well, get over it," he says, at last.

I just look at him.

"What do you think I've been trying to do?" I say.

"Don't give me that," he says, and now Andy is looking me right in the eyes, daring me to disagree.

"What?" I say. "It's true."

"You weren't trying to get over it on Saturday," he says.

I start to say something, but I stop. He's right. He's just standing there, staring at me.

"I was trying to get *away* from it," I say.

"Exactly," he says. That's check and mate, but Andy doesn't even want to win this one. "Just . . . I don't know . . ." he says. "GET OVER IT."

The cashier cranes his neck to look over at us.

I want to say something. I want to say: Well, I'm trying now. But he knows that. At least I hope he does. I was at practice. I took my cuts. We're both quiet for a little while. The cashier looks away.

"Sour Patch?" Andy says. He is physically addicted to Sour Patch Kids.

"Yeah," I say. I want to say something else, something smart or funny, but I don't. The kind of comeback I need can't be made in a pharmacy.

Chapter 43

I'm at practice on Thursday. A few weeks ago, that would have been like saying, "The sun came up this morning," but now it really means something. I feel like I'm sort of back in that rhythm, at least a little bit. One other thing: It's my last chance to get my starting spot back before this week's game.

We start out in the field, throwing baseballs into the big garbage can. It's a little awkward because there are too many of us in the field, and so, of course, Geoff and I both run straight out to left. There's a younger kid out there between us, but we tell him to get lost, and he gets lost all the way to right.

Then it's just the two of us. Geoff is shaded toward center, and I'm over toward the line. We're splitting the difference, ten feet apart. Neither of us says anything, but we know the deal. Anything hit to my right is mine, and anything hit to his left is his. Anything in between will be like three question marks in a row.

Coach Liu starts hitting fungoes. First he hits some choppers to the infield. I just watch. You can really see the difference between our best players and the rest of the kids crowding the infield.

Coach Liu hits one toward short, and two kids hesitate for a second and then charge toward it. They practically collide when they get there, but one of them manages to knock it down with his thigh. He picks it up and chucks it in the general direction of home plate. Coach Liu is standing off to the side of the barrel, but he still has to skip out of the way to avoid being hit in the shins.

He hits the next one to the same place. Maybe he's giving those two another chance to get it right. More likely, he wants them to see how it's done. Katie does her part. The other two hesitate again, leaning back and trying to figure out where and how the ball will bounce. But Katie charges forward as soon as it's hit. She cuts right between them, scoops it up on the short hop, and fires a one-hopper into the square plastic mouth of the can.

She turns around and jogs back, her hat down low and her mouth working some gum. She doesn't say anything to the other two, but her glove just said: What are you doing in my spot? One shades over toward second, the other takes a few steps closer to third.

Then Coach Liu starts lifting fly balls to the outfield.

The first few go to center. I reach up to adjust my cap and reach down to smack my glove once.

The first shot to left isn't to me. Almost as soon as it's hit, I can tell it's heading toward Geoff's side of the field. The extra kid in center starts running for it, too.

"I got it," shouts Geoff. "Mine."

The other kid backs off, and Geoff makes a clean catch. It's a little unusual, because normally the center fielder makes the call, but that kid isn't really the center fielder. He's just the other guy standing there. Manny doesn't mind the company. His spot is secure, and he gets to do plenty of running out there in games. Geoff's throw to the cutoff man is right on target.

A little while later, one comes to my side. It's high and short, an easy play all around. I glove it and then have a short throw to Andy, who has his arms up as the cutoff man. It's almost short enough to try to make the throw home myself. But Andy is in a perfect position and has that accurate infielder's arm.

I make a quick short throw to him as Coach Liu is turning the mouth of the barrel down the third-base line. Andy spins and buries the ball in there on the fly.

It was the right decision, but I jog back to my spot second-guessing myself anyway. It would've been more impressive if I'd delivered a long throw myself. I'm not the starter. I need to win the position. Then again, I don't want another one of those dive-for-it moments.

After that, and I swear Liu does this on purpose: He hits one right in between Geoff and me. And so of course we both end up calling each other off.

"I got it."

"I got it!"

"Got it."

"Got it!"

"Mine."

"Mine!"

But it's a little closer to Geoff, and I let him have it. Again: right decision. Again: I second-guess it.

We do some more drills, and I do OK. What can I do? They're just drills. The best you can do is do them right. I do, and so does Geoff. So, basically, he wins.

Malfoy is slinking around practice all day, but he doesn't say anything to me, and I definitely don't say anything to him.

And then it's time for live pitching. J.P. will probably face half a dozen of us, and there's no guarantee that I'll be one of them. I got a hit off of him last time, though. I'm hoping that will be reason enough to give me another shot. Man, I think back to that day. Everything was just good then. I had no idea I'd be standing out here now, desperately needing to cash in that single for one more shot.

Instead, Coach calls Geoff in. I run out to take his spot in left before anyone else does. Then I stand there not really knowing what to think. I don't want to root against him. He's my teammate and a good guy. None of this is his fault.

I root against him anyway. What? J.P. is my teammate, too.

At least I have enough class not to react when he strikes out. Coach gives him another shot, and he grounds out. He hits it sharply but right to Jackson. J.P. busts it off the mound to cover first, but Jackson takes it himself. He jogs over and easily beats Geoff to the bag.

I'm still concentrating on not smiling when Coach shouts, "Mogens, get in here!"

Yes! He remembered.

It's not till I'm in the on-deck circle timing J.P. that the flip side of that occurs to me. If Coach remembers my hit last time, you can bet J.P. does, too. The next fastball comes in crazy fast, and my pulse revs up another gear.

Dustin is down to the last strike of his second at-bat. I take my right hand off the bat and shake it out to stay loose. I hold it flat and see what I already knew: It's shaking. I put it back on the bat before anyone else can see.

Then Dustin strikes out swinging, and I'm up. My hand is shaking and my pulse is racing. So, of course, J.P. buries the first pitch way inside. The ball doesn't hit me, but an explosion goes off inside me anyway. All I can do is try to concentrate. The next one is inside, too. It's borderline, but Coach gives it to him.

I knew this would happen. Everyone will pitch me this way until I prove I can hit it. And one thing's for sure: I won't get a hit if I don't swing. I make up my mind to swing at the next pitch, no matter what.

I swing over a pitch in the dirt. J.P. is thinking right along with me. Just like that, I'm behind in the count, 1–2. Now I know how the guy in my back pocket must've felt, right before they rolled Chuck's Wagon out of the big leagues.

The next pitch is inside again. I don't swing, and Coach gives me the call this time: 2–2.

"Knock off the junk!" Andy shouts from third.

J.P. looks over at him for a long second. Andy just pounds his glove and looks back at him.

It's so unusual to have the third baseman yell at his own pitcher that Coach makes a noise behind the plate. It's the kind of noise Nax makes in his sleep. I take the opportunity to go through my routine, nice and slow, but I still have some time. J.P. shakes his head, looks in, and goes into his windup.

What the heck, I think, everyone else is talking around here. "Sometimes you squash the bug," I say under my breath.

The pitch comes in, inside but definitely a strike. I put a swing on it and hit a sharp grounder to first. Jackson takes it himself.

Coach doesn't give me another at-bat. I'm glad I put a decent swing on the ball, and maybe he is, too, but we both know I'll be starting Saturday on the bench. I just have to be ready, I tell myself as I put the bat back in the rack. I just have to be ready.

Chapter
44

I think a lot of kids like Saturday because they can sleep in. Me, I'm up earlier than I have been all week. I'm padding around my room in socks because Mom and Dad like to sleep in on the weekends. And since their idea of "sleeping in" means maybe eight thirty, it doesn't seem like so much to ask.

Still, it sort of limits my options. I look over at my computer. I haven't killed a soldier in days. (But I like to think that they're still talking about the bloody rampage I went on last week!) I guess I could play it with the sound off. I'm not really in the mood, but I turn the computer on anyway.

There's a big whopping zippo in my e-mail in-box. Of course, Mom and Dad have so many filters on this thing, it's a wonder anything gets through. Like, St. Paul the

Apostle could send me a personal e-mail telling me to study hard, and it would end up in the spam folder.

I check the spam folder. Nothing from any saints, angels, or celestial beings, but I find some funny stuff that Mom and Dad would probably not be too happy about.

After that, I click on my games. I stay off the battlefield and play a puzzle game instead. At eight fifteen, I get a text from Andy. As I'm answering that, I get another one from Tim. At least I'm not the only one up early. Tim has news, too: "CampL team at batting cages last nt. THREE big guys now!!!!"

"Any1 pitching?" I type.

"Not @ batting cage! LOL!" says Tim.

I get another text from Andy: "Did U hear?"

"Yep. 3! What R they feedin em?"

"Campbells Soup!!!!!!!"

Then one from Tim: "Andy sez they R feeding em Campbells Soup!!!"

And then I hear movement downstairs.

I punch in "CU there!!!!" because the game is on the lumpy little field in Campbeltown. I wish I really felt four exclamation points' worth of excitement. I send it to both of them.

Andy: "CU"

Tim: "L8R"

Then I head downstairs. No surprise, they're in the kitchen. I grab for some Pop-Tarts, but Mom is too quick.

"No way, honey bunchkins," she says, pretending to slap my hand away from the cupboard.

"You're gonna need the good stuff today," says Dad. "I'm thinkin' bacon and eggs."

"The 'good stuff' really isn't all that good for you, you know?" I say. "We learned in science that —"

Dad cuts me off by making that motorboat sound with his lips. "Gives you energy. Campbeltown has three big kids and a bunch of good hitters."

"How do you know that?" I say, though I sort of know.

"The Lu-Lus were over at Hungry Hut last night. Said it was quite a scene at the cages."

"You really shouldn't call them that because —"

But Dad cuts me off with more motorboating. Mom is just smiling and pouring orange juice.

It's funny, they love game day as much as I do. Right now, they probably love it more, but I'm glad. I remember how tense it was on the couch the other night. It's all gone now, washed away by orange juice and motorboats. And all I have to do is step to the plate a few times today and get hit in whatever body part the pitcher feels is appropriate.

Three big kids, I think: the two from last year and a new one? Or, who knows, one from last year and the Monster Beefoid Twins? Whatever the case, there's a pretty good chance one of them will be pitching. I'm not a fan of big pitchers. The name floats through my head: Tebow.

"Hey," says Dad. "Hey!"

It occurs to me, sort of vaguely, that he's been asking me something.

"Earth to honey bunchkins!" Mom says.

That snaps me out of it. "DO NOT call me that at the game!" I say.

"Call you what?" she says. She's always trying to trick me into saying it.

"You know what," I say. "HB."

I'm completely serious, but Mom thinks it's the funniest thing she's heard all morning.

"Sausage or bacon?" Dad says. I guess that's what he was asking.

I give him a look to let him know what a dumb question that is.

"Bacon it is," he says.

As I turn to leave, I hear him say something else, quieter.

"Good to have you back."

Chapter

45

When we get to the field in Campbeltown, Mom and Dad head for the bleachers, and I head for the far side of the field.

"Bet you'll be chomping at the bit," Dad says, right before we split up. He knows I'll be coming off the bench. I never mentioned it, but I guess it's pretty obvious. I don't even really know what that expression means, but it sounds about right. And then he says, "If anyone asks —"

"Family emergency," I say, looking down and watching my feet walk themselves.

"Got it," he says.

I look up in time to see him add in a little wink.

"Go get 'em," Mom begins. I'm afraid she's going to call me HB again. We're close to the bleachers now, and there are parents and kids all around us. "Tiger," she says.

And then I'm free and walking across the grass. Mom and Dad have been cool today, but it's players and coaches only out here, and I like that. I walk in a wide semicircle around the area where the Campbeltown players are warming up. They're the Pirates, by the way. I'm not sure why we don't call them that more. Pirates vs. Braves . . . it's a classic National League matchup.

I look over, trying not to be too obvious. They've definitely got some big kids. And there are a few kids I recognize from years ago. A few of them were teammates of mine as far back as T-ball. I'll probably always recognize them. Isn't that weird?

"Heads up, dingus!" I hear.

I scramble to put my glove on as I look up. I catch sight of the ball a split second before it gets to me and make the catch stepping back.

"What," I say to Andy, "no hello?"

Andy just smirks and points straight up in the air.

I throw it underhand, as high as I can. He camps under it, shuffling his feet, gauging the sun, and making the catch.

As soon as he looks over, I point straight up. It's a sunny day. That's more of a problem for me than for him. Once I get in the game, anyway.

"Nice of you to toss it around with a bench-warmer," I say.

"Yeah," he says. "I'm a real saint."

"Bring it in here!" Coach bellows, and we do.

And then, there's no good way to put this, I find a spot on the bench. Everyone jockeys for the spot at the end, closest to Coach. (Of course, being on the bench mostly means hanging off the fence, but location still matters.) You want him to see you all the time and maybe put you in early.

But Malfoy gets to the best spot first, and I don't want to sit (or hang) next to him. I end up halfway down the bench, looking out at the field through the wire. I just have to trust that Coach won't forget about me. That, and try to make eye contact whenever possible.

We're the away team, obviously, so we start at the plate. We're all waiting for their pitcher to take the mound, and we're glad when he does. He's not that big, maybe just a little above average. But once he starts to throw, I can see he has decent stuff. I hear the first few pitches slap into the catcher's glove, and my pulse starts to race.

Come on, Jack, I tell myself. How much would it even hurt to get hit by this kid?

Then from somewhere deep inside, from some part of myself that I hate, I hear the answer. Plenty, it says, if he hits you in the head.

But I'm watching him warm up, and it looks like he's got good control. I can see him moving the ball around. It should be calming me down, but every time he throws one inside it's like a poke in the gut.

Morgan is a few spots down the bench. I see the kid next to him lean over and say something to him, but I can't quite hear it. Morgan leans forward and catches my eye. "This guy's their ace," he says. "Really good."

I nod and then pass the information down.

The next pitch slaps into the catcher's mitt, louder this time. A little fear is good, I tell myself. Just let me get up there and get it over with. But I've got a long wait, and who knows what a little fear in the first inning will be by the third or fourth? Could even be a big, beefy reliever with a rocket arm and no control by then.

Finally, the game starts and I have something to watch. Three quick outs: not a great start.

"You're chasing!" Coach yells as the starters get their gloves and take the field. "You gotta lay off that junk!"

Coach is subbing in right field from the get-go. As soon as he sends Chester out there to start the game, you know it's probably going to be two innings a pop from then on out. I mean, Chester's not even really an out-fielder. I start to think maybe he'll put me in right to start the third.

I'm half right, because it's a short day for Chester. The Pirates' starter is really locating his pitches today, and that little strike zone doesn't help Chester at all. But it's Malfoy who takes his place: back to his usual spot. That's not cool. Didn't he hit all those kids last game? Shouldn't he be punished more for that?

I give Coach a look, trying to fit all the injustice and wrong in the world into my eyes. He ignores me.

Pitchers' duels go fast. And they go faster when you're on the bench, counting the outs. It's still scoreless in the middle of the third. Coach makes some more substitutions, but I'm not one of them.

When I see Morgan go in, I stick my head in my glove and swear into the leather. No offense, but I mean, seriously. It feels like I'm being punished. It feels like Coach doesn't trust me at all, and I stop trying to make eye contact with him. He'll have to put me in soon anyway, just to get me the required number of outs in the field.

The Pirates get a run in the bottom of the inning. It's not really J.P.'s fault. It starts off with a walk, and OK, technically that is his fault, but it's just a walk. Then the guy advances on two straight groundouts and scores on a bloop hit to shallow right.

We're down 1–0, and I'm still not in the game. I'm feeling pretty useless, and my head is down the next time Coach walks by me.

"Get ready," he says.

"Whuzzat, Coach?" I say.

"Putting you in for the rest of the game," he says. "Was holding you out for a reason."

And I guess I'm still not making the connection, so he makes it for me.

"Tight game, and you can hit this guy."

All of a sudden, I understand. Subbing is an art in Little League. I mean, ideally, you build up a big lead and then get everyone in during garbage time. But how often does that really happen? In these close games, you can't just run all your worst players out for the last two innings, not if you want to win. Sometimes you might want to save a surprise for the other team. Like, say, a kid who was a starter two weeks ago.

"OK," I say as I get to my feet.

I look out at the field, and it's like I'm seeing it clearly for the first time all day. It's a close ball game, a sunny day, and my coach doesn't think I'm useless after all.

I'm in the field for the bottom of the fourth. Nothing comes my way, but I keep my head in the game. I wait until Manny hauls in the third out before I start really concentrating on my at-bat. I'm leading off the top of the fifth, and their starter is still going strong. When I said before that he wasn't that big, I was missing one obvious thing: He's about the same size as J.P.

The inning starts and I step to the plate.

"What's his name?" I ask their catcher as I step in. They've been calling it all game long, but all I could make out was a lot of vowels.

"Wooster," the catcher says. "Jamie Wooster. We call him Woosh."

I go through my full routine. It's the start of the inning, so there's time. I'm doing anything I can to avoid thinking about the baseball, about Woosh coming inside, and about how pitchers can lose control when they get tired. But it's hard to fool yourself with your own tricks.

So, yeah, I'm freaking out a little. You know the symptoms; I won't repeat 'em. What's happening on the field is a lot more important than what's happening in my head. We're down by one run to the Campbeltown Pirates, we've got six outs to get it done, and I've waited all game for this shot.

The windup . . . and the pitch.

I can see right away that it's outside. I think about swinging at it anyway, just because it's outside and I can. But that's dumb. You don't swing at a pitch out of relief. I let it go, and the ump does the right thing.

I'm a new batter, and Woosh was just sizing me up. Now he's behind, and I figure he'll come right at me. I take my mini swings, and he goes into his windup.

I can feel the sweat under my batting glove, and I can hear my pulse. And he hasn't even come inside yet. The longer this goes on, the worse I'll get. And there's no way a control pitcher is going to want to fall behind 2–0. It all adds up to one thing.

The ball is cutting in toward me, but my bat is already moving. There's nowhere for me to go and nothing for me to do except hit the thing. The contact feels good. It's in toward my hands but solid. Before I even look up, I know I've hit this one on a rope . . .

. . . right to the third baseman. He makes a good play and catches it on the fly. One out.

Ugh. An at-'em ball. If I hadn't started so early, maybe I could've squeezed it in between third and short. I head back to the bench. Nothing I can do about it now. I get my glove and stand by the fence.

"Good swing, man," says Andy.

"Tough break," says Tim.

"Bad luck," says Dustin.

Five outs left, still down by one. All I can do is hope I get another shot.

Chapter 46

We get a bloop single and a walk in the fifth but leave them both stranded. Once I get positioned in left, I do the math to figure out what it will take for me to get another shot at the plate. I need two of the guys in front of me to reach base.

It's possible. Woosh might be getting tired or he might not be. His pitch count isn't as high as it should be because we've been swinging at too many first pitches. We'll hear about that next week. It's tough, though. He's been around the plate, and his stuff looks hittable. He's just keeping us off balance.

Yeah, we got two base runners in the fifth, but the single was just barely over the second baseman's glove, and the walk was borderline. And then J.P. goes into his windup, and I focus on the plate.

J.P. is really battling. I gotta say: He looks a little tired himself. Even from out here, I can see that his fastball doesn't have the same pop on it. I stay ready and watch him work. Sometimes a tired pitcher means a lot of work for the left fielder. Even tired, though, J.P. is something else. He's doing what their pitcher has been doing: getting ahead in the count, keeping the batters guessing.

He strikes out the first guy with a ball in the dirt. The kid heads back to the dugout bopping himself on his helmet with the bat. Been there.

The next batter hits a slow dribbler and beats it out for an infield single. There's one on, one out, and one of their big kids coming up.

J.P. takes a little extra time, then goes into his windup and throws a pitch I didn't even know he had. Ahead 0–1, he wastes a pitch way outside. The kid doesn't chase, even though it looks like he has the reach to get to it. The count is 1–1, but it turns out it wasn't a wasted pitch after all. The big kid is looking outside now, and J.P. ties him up with junk on the inside half. It's 1–2, and now J.P. has the whole plate to play with. He reaches back for his best fastball of the last two innings and strikes him out swinging.

Two outs with a runner on first and an ace who still has something in the tank: You can almost feel the other team deflate a little, glad they still have that 1–0 lead. The next kid chops a routine grounder to short. Katie is back in the game after being subbed early. She gobbles it up and flips it to second for the easy out.

We head in to bat. We're still down by a run, but most of our starters are back in now, and it's the top of the order. Tim is batting leadoff. In a textbook example of how not to start a rally, he pops the first pitch straight up. Their catcher throws off his mask, waits for it, and makes the play. One out.

Then Manny starts fouling off pitches. The strike zone has four edges: inside, outside, knees, and letters. Woosh is working all four and hitting more often than he misses. But Manny spoils the good ones and takes the bad ones. Nine pitches later, he trots down to first. We all cheer.

"Good eye, Manimal!" shouts Dustin.

"Radar locked!" yells Chester.

Manny just lets out a long breath. Walks like that are hard work.

Jackson steps to the plate. Just looking at him you can see that he has power, and Woosh is careful with him and falls behind in the count. Finally, he has to give him something over the plate. Jackson puts a good swing on it, and I think this might be it. But he's just underneath and lifts it to center. Manny doesn't risk tagging up, and now we're the team with two outs and a runner on first. The difference: We don't have a lead to fall back on.

Andy steps to the plate. His first game in the cleanup spot hasn't gone well so far. He taps his cleats with the bat and stares out at the mound. It's his last shot and mine, too. If he doesn't reach base, the game is over.

"Come on, Andy!" I shout from the on-deck circle. "Come on, man!"

I can hear my pulse thundering in my ears. It started as soon as I put the batting helmet on, but at this point, I can't tell if it's fear that I'll have to bat or fear that I won't.

Over by the bench my teammates are cheering. Morgan and some of the other younger kids have their hats on inside out as rally caps. But all that matters is what Andy does at the plate. He gets a pitch to hit: pretty fast but fat. He's late on it and fouls it back. The second pitch gets a lot of the plate, too, but he doesn't take the bat off his shoulders.

He's tight, I think. It's not hard for me to recognize the signs these days. I wish there was something I could do about it.

"Come on, dingus!" I shout.

I don't know if he hears me. Sometimes you don't hear anything when you're at the plate, and sometimes you hear everything. Whatever the case, his bat comes forward this time. With the count 0–2, you wouldn't think the pitch would be anywhere near the strike zone. But Woosh must want to get this over with, because he throws a changeup over the plate. It's a bad pitch because his fast-ball isn't as fast now, so there's not as much difference with the change.

Andy puts a swing on this one.

Lucky or good, which would you choose? Andy hits the lamest dying duck of a flare over the shortstop's head. It's coming down slowly but tailing away. Three different players — the shortstop, third baseman, and left fielder — look like they might have a shot at it. None of them quite get there. The thing lands in the grass between them and doesn't even bounce.

Manny was running on contact with two outs and makes it to second easily. They don't even bother with a throw to first. It's such a weird play that it takes me a few seconds to realize that I'm up. Then it hits me like a tidal wave, and all I can do is direct my feet toward the plate and hope they know the way.

There are so many things I could think about. There's the game situation: We're behind by one and down to our final out. There are faceless nightmare pitchers and nasty real ones. I don't have to look farther than the on-deck circle to see Malfoy. Woosh owned him last at-bat, so hitting me wouldn't even be such a bad play for him.

There are trips to the hospital and "maybe minor concussions" and my parents in the stands and a dozen other things. And so you know what? I decide not to think about any of them. Here's what I think: I think you've got to have a routine. I think that all the big leaguers on TV do, so I do, too.

I dig my front foot in. You know what I'm thinking about when I'm digging my foot in? I'm thinking about digging my foot in. Then I sit down on my back leg and take my practice swings.

Then the pitch comes in, and it's junk, and I don't swing at it. And even though the count's just 1–0, I know he's not going to want to fall any further behind. I know he wants this game over with. Not me. I realize this right then: I want another run. I *want* another at-bat.

Woosh takes some extra time, just like J.P. did last inning. He goes into his windup, and I feel that same panic. There's nothing I can do about it, but as a wise man once said: Get over it.

The pitch is inside half . . . but it's a changeup. I have time to react and put a swing on it. I don't try to do too much. I just want to make a nice level swing, and that's what I do.

It's amazing how far those can go. I feel the contact: solid and sweet. I know it's headed for deep center before I even look up. Two weeks ago, I would've stood there and watched it for a few seconds, like they do on TV.

Not now: I bust it out of the box. I have my head down and I'm hauling. I take a quick look out to center but don't catch sight of the ball right away. As I near first, I look over and see Manny booking around third, heading for home. Andy is past second.

I look out and see the center fielder backpedaling as fast as he can. And then I see the ball and put my head back down. I've been playing outfield a long time, and as fast as their center fielder is moving, it's not going to be fast enough. Heading toward second, I see Meacham coaching third. His arm is going like a propeller: Go! Go! Go!

It's a two-run triple, and it gives us the lead. I don't even know what to do once I get to third. Triples don't grow on trees — and this one almost never happened. I feel like shouting, but I don't. I feel like passing out, but I don't do that, either. If I fell off the base, they could tag me out. I look around instead.

Katie is loosening up along the sideline. She tilts her cap up, and I see the flash of her eyes. For a second, we're looking right at each other. Then she touches the tip of her nose with one finger. I smile: Hit it on the nose.

Coach Meacham comes up and pats me on the back. He's downright friendly for about twelve seconds, which has to be a personal record. Then his son pops out to short. "Pathetic," he spits.

I head in to get my glove and half the team smacks me on the head before I can get my batting helmet off. It occurs to me that I could get a minor concussion just from this, but it feels great.

"YESSSS!" says Andy before smashing both of his palms down on my poor helmet.

"This is all you, man," I shout at him.

He probably thinks I mean because his hit kept the inning alive. But that's only half of it. We both have a job to do now, though. We grab our gloves on the fly. We still have the bottom half of the inning to go.

Of course, there's one other thing we've still got. J.P. intercepts me on my way out to left. He should really be on the mound already, but he's here running alongside me. He doesn't say anything, just taps my shoulder with his glove. I smile and tap him back.

As he goes into his windup a few minutes later, his face turns toward left. The infielders are already looking in, so I'm probably the only one who sees the little smile on his face. And that smile says plenty. It says, My teammate has given me another shot at this one. My head-case, 'fraid-o'-the-ball teammate has given me another shot. And then he turns and fires. That pitch, crisp as the first inning, says something else. It says, I got this.

I allow myself to look around as the ump calls the strike. I see my parents in the bleachers, leaning in for the call. I see the sun flash off the bronze of Katie's pony-tail as she takes a step to the side. And I see the green grass all around me: left field, my spot. I got this.

ABOUT THE AUTHOR

Michael Northrop spent twelve years chasing stories for *Sports Illustrated Kids*, the last five of those as baseball editor. His first novel, *Gentlemen*, earned him a *Publishers Weekly* Flying Start citation for a notable debut, and his second, *Trapped*, was an Indie Next List selection. He has also written short fiction for *Weird Tales*, the *Notre Dame Review*, and *McSweeney's*. He now writes full-time from his home in New York City. You can visit Michael online at www.michaelnorthrop.net.